THE TRAILSMAN: WYOMING WIPEOUT

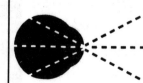

This Large Print Book carries the
Seal of Approval of N.A.V.H.

THE TRAILSMAN: WYOMING WIPEOUT

JON SHARPE

WHEELER PUBLISHING

An imprint of Thomson Gale, a part of The Thomson Corporation

THOMSON

™

GALE

Detroit • New York • San Francisco • New Haven, Conn. • Waterville, Maine • London

THOMSON

GALE

LIBRARY OF CONGRESS CATALOGING-IN-PUBLICATION DATA

Sharpe, Jon.
   [Wyoming wipeout]
   The trailsman : Wyoming wipeout / by Jon Sharpe.
     p. cm. — (Wheeler Publishing Large Print Western.)
   ISBN-13: 978-1-59722-574-8 (softcover : alk. paper)
   ISBN-10: 1-59722-574-6 (softcover : alk. paper)
   1. Fargo, Skye (Fictitious character) — Fiction. 2. Wyoming — Fiction.
   3. Large type books. I. Title.
   PS3561.N645W96 2007
   813'.54—dc22
                                    2007015813

Published in 2007 by arrangement with NAL Signet,
a member of Penguin Group (USA) Inc.

Printed in the United States of America on permanent paper
10 9 8 7 6 5 4 3 2 1

Fort Laramie, 1858 — there's a dangerous gang of stagecoach robbers on the loose along the mail route, and only the Trailsman can stop them. If they don't kill him first.

1

Skye Fargo wasn't looking for a job. He'd just gotten into St. Joseph, and he had a little money to spend. He figured on staying in town and enjoying himself for a day or so before looking for some pilgrims to escort along the Oregon Trail to Fort Laramie, Fort Bridger, or all the way to Oregon if that was what they wanted.

So when the little man in dude's clothes showed up at his elbow, Fargo told him to go away.

"I'm afraid I can't do that," the man said. He might have been a little fella, but he had a big voice that carried well in the noisy room. "You *are* Skye Fargo aren't you? The one they call the Trailsman?"

Fargo was tempted to lie, but he didn't think it would do any good. He said, "That's me."

"And I am Samuel Dobkins. You are the man I am looking for."

Dobkins had a soft, round face and a thick black mustache. He wore white checkered pants and a purple checked frock coat. On his head was a straw topper with a black band. The hat added nearly a foot to his inconsiderable height. He didn't look like anybody who'd be interested in a trip to Oregon.

"I don't know you," Fargo said, hoping Dobkins would go away.

Dobkins didn't leave. He touched the brim of his topper and said, "Mr. Ferriday wants to talk to you."

Fargo was more interested in the glass of whiskey on the table in front of him than in somebody named Mr. Ferriday. He said so.

"Mr. J. M. Ferriday," Dobkins said.

Fargo shook his head. The name was familiar, but he wasn't interested in talking to anyone. "I still don't care."

"That's neither here nor there," the dude said. "The fact remains that you simply must go talk to Mr. Ferriday. At once."

Fargo sighed and looked around the saloon. Men laughed and talked at the tables, and a couple of card games were going on near the wall to one side. The bar was lined with men who had nowhere better to go and nothing better to do. Fargo wished he was one of them instead of sitting there talking to Dobkins.

"Show's starting in a few minutes," Fargo said, gesturing toward the tiny stage at the rear of the big room. "I'm planning to see it."

"You can return this evening," Dobkins told him. "There will be another show."

Fargo took a drink of his whiskey. It was bad whiskey, but it was better than no whiskey at all. He set the glass back on the table and said, "I don't want to come back this evening, and I don't want to talk to Mr. Ferriday. Now light a shuck."

Dobkins straightened his shoulders and tugged at his coat to straighten it. He opened his mouth, but he didn't have a chance to say anything because a large, snaggletoothed man with a mug of beer in each hand walked by and deliberately knocked off Dobkins' hat with one elbow.

The man laughed loudly and went on his way. Dobkins picked up his hat, dusted it off, and set it firmly on his head.

"Excuse me, Mr. Fargo," he said, turning to follow the man who'd knocked off his hat.

The man was about to sit down at a table with three others when Dobkins caught up with him.

"You did that deliberately," Dobkins said.

Setting the beer mugs on the table, Snaggletooth turned to face him. "Yeah? And so what if I did?"

He was a good foot taller than Dobkins, even counting the topper. Dobkins looked at him for a second and then kicked him in the knee. The man wasn't bothered any more than if a mosquito had bitten him. He swept Dobkins' hat off with a hand the size of a frying pan. The hat sailed a couple of feet and hit the floor near another table.

Dobkins went over to pick up the hat. When he reached for it, Snaggletooth crushed it to the floor with his foot.

Dobkins whirled and slammed a fist into the man's groin. The man buckled, and Dobkins head-butted him, smashing his nose. Blood flew.

The man's three friends jumped up from the table and lunged at Dobkins. All around, people shoved back their chairs and tables and got out of the way, ready to watch Dobkins get dismembered.

Fargo sighed. It wasn't his fight, and it wasn't his fault, but he didn't feel he could sit by and watch Dobkins get beaten. Dobkins had come there looking for him, after all, and the little man had grit.

Fargo hoped Dobkins' attackers would listen to reason, but just in case they wouldn't, he pulled his gun.

"I don't allow any gunplay in here," the bartender said at Fargo's back.

Fargo glanced around. The bartender held a shotgun, and it was pointed at the Trailsman.

"They'll tear the place up," Fargo said.

The bartender shrugged, but the gun remained steady. "If they do, they'll pay for it. Now holster that hogleg."

Fargo did as he was told. By that time Dobkins was at the bottom of a pile of squirming men and flying fists.

"Be all right if I joined in?" Fargo said.

The bartender grinned. "Be my guest."

The snaggletoothed man who'd started the whole thing was in a dither. He didn't know whether to hold his bleeding nose or his injured gonads. Fargo shoved him to a seat in an empty chair and pulled one man off the pile. The man windmilled his arms in an attempt to hit Fargo, but the Trailsman avoided the futile blows. He took the man by the shirtfront and belt, and heaved him over a table. He hit headfirst on the floor, rolled over, and was still.

A second man jumped up and grabbed a chair. He broke it across Fargo's back before the Trailsman could turn around. Fargo stumbled forward and fell into the table that he'd tossed the first man over. The table collapsed under his weight. The men sitting there just scooted their chairs back out of the way as the second man pounced for Fargo.

The Trailsman flipped over before the man reached him and got his hands up in time to put them around his attacker's throat. The man's fingers gouged at Fargo's eyes, but Fargo's grip tightened. The man's face reddened and his breath rasped, then whistled, then stopped. His hands fell limp, and Fargo pushed him aside.

When he stood up, he was surprised to see Dobkins standing over the third man. Dobkins held the leg of the chair that had been broken across Fargo's back in both hands, like a club, and he must have used it like one. The last man's hair hung bloody and matted over his forehead.

As Fargo watched, Dobkins tossed the chair leg on the man's chest and dusted himself off. He straightened his frock coat and looked around for his hat. When he saw it, he bent over and picked it up. He shook it off and punched it out with his fist. It was battered and dirty, but Dobkins put it on.

The snaggletooth who'd started it all still sat in the chair where Fargo had pushed him. He held a dirty cloth to his bloody nose and had one hand in his crotch.

Fargo walked back to his table and tossed down the rest of his whiskey. He put down the glass and saw that Dobkins was standing beside him.

"Are you ready to go, Mr. Fargo?" Dobkins said.

"I'm not going."

"After all my trouble? You certainly are."

Fargo started to repeat his previous comment when he felt something jab his side. Glancing down he saw that Dobkins was poking a derringer into his ribs.

"Well?" Dobkins said.

"I guess I might as well go with you," Fargo said.

Dobkins nodded. "I thought you might. After you, Mr. Fargo."

Fargo led the way toward the door. Just before he pushed through the bat-wings, the bartender called to them. "Who's paying for the damages?"

Dobkins gestured over his shoulder with his thumb to where the men lay. "They are."

"Sure enough," the bartender said.

Dobkins jabbed Fargo with the derringer again. "Keep moving, Mr. Fargo," he said.

Fargo kept moving.

2

The office of J. M. Ferriday was a bit different from the saloon. A massive oak desk sat in the middle of the room on a carpeted floor. Green curtains hung at the sides of the windows, and the chairs were upholstered with green-and-white-striped fabric. A pen holder sat on the desk beside a thick ledger book.

Ferriday himself sat behind the desk. He rose as Fargo entered the room with Dobkins close behind.

"You must be Mr. Fargo," Ferriday said, leaning over the desk and extending his hand. "When I send Dobkins to find someone, he never fails to accomplish the task."

Fargo shook hands with Ferriday and said that he wasn't surprised.

Dobkins removed his hat, smiled modestly, and said nothing. The derringer had disappeared somewhere inside his checked coat.

Ferriday was dressed in more businesslike attire than his associate. His frock coat and pants were black, as was the tie he wore. His hair was black as well, though streaked with gray. His face was lean and unlined, with a thin slash of a mouth. He looked to Fargo like a man who kept a close eye on his money.

"Have a seat, Mr. Fargo," Ferriday said.

Fargo sat in one of the upholstered chairs. "Make it just plain Fargo," he said.

"As you wish," Ferriday said, sitting behind his desk and clasping his hands on top of it. "I don't suppose Dobkins mentioned what I wanted to discuss with you."

"No," Fargo said. "He didn't get the chance. But he was persuasive."

Dobkins grinned but remained silent. He had taken a seat in the chair near the one where Fargo sat, and his feet barely reached the floor.

"He's a smooth talker, all right," Ferriday said, "but I instructed him not to say any more than was absolutely necessary in this case. I didn't want word getting out that I might be hiring you for a specific purpose."

"I'm not looking for a job," Fargo told him.

"Perhaps not. But I think you're just the man for the one I have to offer. I can promise you that you will be well compensated for it."

While Fargo wasn't really interested, he didn't like to pass up a good opportunity. He said, "Just exactly what did you have in mind for me to do?"

"Do you know what my business is?"

"You have the mail line for the Oregon Trail," Fargo said.

"That's correct."

"I don't drive a stage," Fargo said. He could if he had to, and he'd done it before, but never as a steady job.

Ferriday nodded. "You wouldn't have to. I know quite a bit about you, Fargo, and I don't need a stage driver. I need a man with a different kind of talent."

Fargo had been a scout, and he'd led wagon trains. He'd done a lot of things along those lines. "Which talent would that be, exactly?"

"I need someone who's familiar with the territory around Fort Laramie. Someone who's not afraid of a bit of danger and who knows what to do when there's trouble."

"He knows about that, all right," Dobkins said, speaking for the first time since entering the office.

"Yes," Ferriday said. "I was wondering about your hat and the dirt on your coat."

Dobkins lifted the hat from his lap and held it up for inspection. "It's a little the worse for wear, sir, but then so is the man who soiled it. Thanks to Mr. Fargo's pitching in at the right moment, I escaped with my life."

Ferriday tut-tutted. "You really should stay out of scrapes, Dobkins. It's not good for the company for its employees to behave like common brawlers."

"Yes, sir," Dobkins said without a trace of repentance in his tone.

Ferriday waved off the obviously insincere apology. "Well, never mind. If what you say is true, it proves that Fargo is the man I need."

"I believe you're right, sir," Dobkins said.

Fargo could have done without the endorsement, but he didn't object. He said, "You said the job wasn't driving a stage, but you haven't said what it is."

"Robbery," Ferriday said.

"I don't go in for that line of work," Fargo said.

Ferriday looked offended. "I didn't mean that you would have to be a robber. Quite the contrary. I need someone to stop the robberies of my mail coach."

"I'm not a lawman, either."

"And I'm not asking you to become one."

"Seems to me we're right back where we started," Fargo said. "You still haven't said what the job is."

"You'll have to pardon me, Fargo." Ferriday gave him a thin smile. "I've become accustomed to talking to businessmen and, with them, circumlocution is the expected manner of discourse."

"If that means what I think it does, I'm not like those businessmen. Let's get to it."

"Very well," Ferriday said. "Dobkins, you may stay and listen." For Fargo's benefit, Ferriday added, "I trust Dobkins completely."

Dobkins grinned and nodded, as if that was something he'd heard before.

"Maybe you're too trusting," Fargo said to Ferriday.

Ferriday nodded. "Could be, but I don't trust just anybody. Dobkins is the only one besides myself, in fact. But I'm about to trust you."

"Why's that?"

"Because, as I said, I know quite a bit about you. Everything I've heard leads me to believe you're a man who can be trusted."

"You can't believe everything you hear. Folks have been known to stretch the truth now and then."

"In this case, I think I can believe them,

since all accounts that I've heard agree about you. Oh, you're no saint. That's pretty clear. But I'm not looking for a saint. One of those wouldn't do for this job. I'm looking for someone who's not afraid of a little danger."

Fargo didn't mind danger, but he didn't like stalling. "You still haven't told me what the job is."

Dobkins, who had been standing quietly by the door, made a noise that might have been a laugh, though it didn't sound much like one.

"All right, Fargo," Ferriday said. "Here it is. Someone's been robbing the mail coaches. I want it stopped. And I think you're the one to stop it."

Fargo couldn't figure why Ferriday was even talking to him about something like that.

"Sounds like that's a job for a federal marshal," he said. "Not me. That's not in my line."

"That doesn't matter. You know what it's like at Fort Laramie."

It wasn't a question, so Fargo didn't answer.

Ferriday continued. "It's the jumping-off place. There's no marshal within a hundred miles, and the government's not going to send one."

"Why not?"

"Because the robbers aren't taking the mail."

Fargo knew the rules of the coach line, and one of them was that they didn't haul valuables, except possibly in the mail. There was a simple reason for that rule: to avoid robberies.

"What are they taking, then?" he asked.

"Money," Ferriday said. "Not from the mail. From the passengers."

Fargo started to say something, but Ferriday held up a hand. "I know what you're thinking. We're not a passenger line. That's true, but we do carry passengers — quite often in fact — and occasionally one of them will be carrying a sum of money. It seems as if these robbers know every time, or almost every time. How, I have no idea. They never stop a coach when there are no passengers or when the passengers have no money to speak of. But every time there's someone with money aboard, there's danger of a robbery." He gave Fargo a straight look. "As I said, I want it stopped."

Fargo wasn't interested. "I don't do that kind of work. I'm not a stage guard. I don't like riding stages."

That was the truth. As far as Fargo was

concerned, there wasn't a single thing to like about riding a coach. From the swaying and the bumps to the crowded compartment to the hard seats, it was all unpleasant and uncomfortable.

"You don't have to ride the stage," Ferriday told him. "I'd pay you well just to go out to Fort Laramie, have a look around, and see if you can figure out what's going on there. Even if you're not successful, you'll still be paid."

Fargo thought it over. It was hard to resist an offer like that.

"If it doesn't work out," Ferriday said, "you can always find people at Laramie who'll pay you to take them on to Bridger or back here to Saint Jo."

He was right about that, Fargo knew. It wasn't as if he couldn't find another job after a week or so of trying what Ferriday was asking him to do.

"Well, Fargo?" Ferriday said.

"You'd be paying me now?" Fargo said. "In advance?"

Ferriday didn't blink. "Of course. I said I trusted you."

Fargo nodded. "All right. I'll give you a week after I get to Laramie. If I haven't come across anything by then, I'll be moving along."

"That sounds fair enough. At least a week, however. Passengers with money don't come along just every day."

A week seemed like a long time to Fargo. When he said so, Ferriday told him how much he was willing to pay. It was a considerable sum.

"A week then," Fargo said, "but not a day longer."

"And how soon can you be on the job?"

Fargo estimated how long it would take him to get to Fort Laramie.

"That's fine. I'd want you to begin looking into things immediately."

Fargo had an uncomfortable feeling that he wasn't getting the whole story from Ferriday, who was offering a lot of money for something that wasn't that much of a problem. If he lost all his passenger business, he wouldn't be losing much revenue.

But Fargo hated to turn down the money. "I can look into it," he said.

Ferriday stood up, and so did Fargo. The two men shook hands again, and Ferriday said, "I have a feeling you're going to take care of things for me, Fargo. I always pick the right man for the job. But be careful. These robbers are dangerous. They haven't killed anyone yet, but it's only a matter of time before they do."

"They won't kill me," Fargo said. "It's been tried before, and it didn't take."

"You know what they say about that."

"No. What do they say?"

"There's always a first time."

Fargo grinned. "It'd be the last time, too, if they did it. But you don't have to worry about me."

"I won't then. Shall we go to the bank and conclude our transaction?"

Fargo said that sounded like a fine idea.

Dobkins hadn't said a word while the conversation was going on. Now he moved aside when Ferriday and Fargo started for the door.

"You can come along, Dobkins," Ferriday told him.

"Yes, sir," Dobkins said.

3

Fargo had been to Fort Laramie a number of times in the course of his travels across the West. It wasn't exactly a fort because there was no stockade enclosing it. One had been planned, or so Fargo had heard, but the government was short of money at the time it was to be built, so it never got done.

Fargo sat astride the big Ovaro stallion he rode and looked down the trail ahead of him. The Laramie River flowed behind the fort, and the Trailsman saw the sun reflect off its surface. He saw the two-story officers' quarters with its whitewashed walls, long balcony, and outside staircase, the soldiers' barracks, the stables, and the tall flagpole.

Outside the official perimeter of the fort, but still within its protection, were other buildings: a couple of saloons, a sutler's store, and two other stores. The sutler dealt mostly with the soldiers, and the other storekeepers were there hoping to make a profit off the pilgrims who came through in the wagon trains.

The saloon owners would make a profit off anyone they could. The soldiers did most of their drinking on the post, but there were plenty of thirsty pilgrims, and not a few even thirstier Indians.

There were several tepees near the fort, as a few Indians always gathered around a fort, not for protection but for other reasons, including the saloons.

The saloons welcomed anybody with the money to buy a drink: cutthroats, cardsharpers, thieves, and killers, as well as the trappers, traders, and pilgrims. Even the Indians were welcomed as customers, though they wouldn't be allowed to drink inside the building. Fargo was a little saddened at the thought. For some Indians he'd known, drinking liquor was the same as drinking poison, but that didn't stop them.

Fargo flicked the reins, and the Ovaro moved forward. Fargo knew he'd better report to the commanding officer, a colonel whose name was Alexander. Alexander was a good man, and Fargo had scouted for him once or twice. They weren't exactly friends, but they trusted each other.

Colonel Alexander wasn't a large man, nowhere near as tall as Fargo, but he had a presence that let you know he wasn't anybody to be trifled with.

"Good afternoon, Fargo," he said, standing as the Trailsman walked into his office. "Haven't seen you around these parts for a while."

"Been elsewhere," Fargo said as the two shook hands. "Things been quiet around here?"

Alexander sat down and motioned for Fargo to take one of the wooden chairs across from the desk.

"You know how it is," Alexander said. "Between the Crow and the Sioux, there's always something for us to attend to."

Fargo waited for him to mention the stage robberies. When he didn't, the Trailsman said, "What about the robberies on the mail run?"

Alexander leaned forward. "How did you know about that?"

Fargo shrugged. "You hear a lot of things in Saint Jo."

"Mr. Ferriday wouldn't like that. It might hurt his business."

Fargo nodded.

"He's been in contact with me, asking me to send a patrol out with his mail coaches. I haven't been able to spare the men except for a time or two, and nothing happened on those occasions."

"Maybe you could put a stop to things if some of the men rode along every time."

"That's true enough," Alexander said. "If I had another fifty men, I might be able to do that." His eyes narrowed. "You're not working for Ferriday, are you?"

Fargo wasn't surprised that Alexander had figured it out so quickly. The colonel hadn't achieved his rank because he was stupid.

"I talked to him," Fargo said. "Told him I wasn't a stage guard."

Alexander thought that over. "What you do out here's your own business. Whatever it is, you don't have any official standing, so I'm not obliged to help you."

Fargo said he understood that and added, "Not that I'm doing anything along the lines you're thinking."

"You always did play your cards close to the vest, Fargo, and that's a good thing. Keeps people from knowing too much about your business. Well, you do what you please, as long as it doesn't interfere with my work here."

"It won't," Fargo said.

"Fine. What's your plan?"

"To have a drink," Fargo said.

The name of the Red Dog Saloon was scrawled in charcoal on a board outside, which gave people stopping by a pretty good idea of the quality of the liquor it served and the kind of people to be found inside. Fargo had been there before, so he already had a pretty good idea.

The place was convenient to the stage stop, practically right next door, so Fargo thought it would be a good place to start looking into things for Ferriday.

Fargo went inside and inhaled the familiar smells of tobacco smoke and beer. He wasn't expecting to find anything out of the ordinary, so he was surprised when he saw the young woman sitting at one of the tables. She had flame red hair, a pretty, heart-shaped face, and a light dusting of freckles across her nose. She was wearing men's denim pants and a work shirt, but what he could see of her figure was as enticing as her face and hair. Maybe even more enticing.

She made the two faded whores who frequented the saloon look like exactly what they were. They sat at a table near the silent old upright piano, looking gloomy and lonesome. The redhead wasn't lonesome at all. Five men were crowded around the table with her, and three or four others were standing as close by as they could.

Fargo couldn't blame the soiled doves if they were a little bit jealous, and he was suddenly glad he'd accepted Ferriday's job. He moved to the bar, where there was plenty of room. Nearly everyone was trying to get near the redhead. A couple of older men who didn't seem interested in her were at the bar, and Fargo stood between them to order a whiskey.

"Haven't seen you around in a while, Fargo," the bartender said as he poured the drink.

"Haven't been around these parts lately." He nodded toward the young woman. "Your customers have gotten a lot better looking since the last time I came by."

He tasted his whiskey. It was just as bad as it had always been.

"She's been good for business," the bartender said before moving away to serve another customer.

"Don't you go gettin' any ideas about her," said the man on Fargo's left.

Fargo turned his head slightly for a look. The man was short and stout, and dirty white hair hung out from under his hat. He hadn't seen soap and water for a while. A long while. "I got my sights on her already."

"You and ever'body else in this godforsaken place," said the man on the right. He was taller and cleaner than the other man, but not by much in either case. "I been comin' in here for three weeks now, hoping for a chance with one of them Coleman sisters, and all I've got is drunk."

"Sisters?" Fargo said.

"That's right. The one there's Faith. There's three more of 'em, and each one's prettier than the other one. They come in now and then, and the men flock around 'em like bees after a flower." He looked at Fargo with rheumy eyes. "You wouldn't buy a man a drink, would you?"

Fargo said that he would. He signaled the bartender, who poured the man a whiskey.

"You're the fella they call the Trailsman, ain't you?" the man said.

Fargo nodded.

"I figgered that. My name's Johnny Cobb. I seen you in here once before. You got into a fight that time."

"I'm not looking for a fight," Fargo said.

"You can find one if you want it," said the man on the left. "Just try shoving into a seat at the table where that gal is."

Cobb downed his drink in a couple of swallows and wiped his mouth.

"Mighty fine," he said, which proved to Fargo that the whiskey had killed his sense of taste. "You don't want to be shovin' in. Old Farley over there tried it once. Got his ass kicked."

Farley, the man on the left, grinned and showed what remained of his teeth.

"What's worse," Cobb said, "is that it was the gal that kicked it."

"She sure as hell did," Farley said. He didn't seem to be embarrassed by it. "Those Coleman sisters is tough."

"No wonder," Cobb said. "Considerin' their old man."

Farley called the bartender over and ordered another whiskey. The bartender looked at Fargo.

"I'm buying," the Trailsman said.

"Then I'll have another one, myself," Cobb said, and tossed down what was left in his glass.

"What about their old man?" Fargo said.

"Samson Coleman," Cobb said. He looked at Fargo. "You're a big one, but Samson's taller'n you, and wider into the bargain. You ever see a grizzly rare up on its hind legs?"

Fargo said he had, more than once.

Cobb nodded. "Figgered you had. Well, then, if you've seen that, you pretty much know what Samson looks like. How he ever got him any daughters like that is a wonder."

"Where'd he come from?" Fargo asked. He'd never heard of Samson before, and he'd been around Laramie often enough.

Farley answered, "Don't anybody know. He and them gals just showed up a while back. They live off from the fort, in the mountains somewhere. Samson don't come down here much himself, but them girls are here pretty often. Sure do brighten the place up."

"But Samson does come around now and then," Fargo said.

"Yep," Cobb said. "Kate Follett over to Follett's Store is a widow now, and Samson's taken a shine to her." He reached in front of Fargo to nudge Farley's elbow. "He ain't the only one, either."

"You shut up, Cobb," Farley said. "She ain't never give me a second look."

Cobb laughed. "Can't blame her, either. An old he-coon like you."

Fargo knew Kate Follett. She was no longer young, but she was a fine figure of a woman. She'd come to Laramie with her husband, who'd started the store, but he'd died of a fever the first winter. Instead of going back east as most women would have done, Kate had stayed to run the store and she'd done a fine job of it. She sounded like the kind of woman a man like Samson would be interested in.

Fargo, however, didn't care about Samson so much as the daughters.

"I guess I'll go make myself acquainted with Miss Coleman," he said.

Cobb raised his whiskey glass and tipped it toward Fargo.

"Good luck to you," he said, but Fargo could tell he didn't really mean it.

4

Samson Coleman thought it was about time he went over to the saloon and fetched his daughter home, but he wanted to stay a few minutes more in Kate Follett's store. He hadn't thought he'd ever want another woman, not after his wife's death, the thought of which was still bitter bile to him even though many years had passed. In spite of his undying love and his bitterness, however, there was something about Kate that he found downright irresistible.

It wasn't just that she was a fine-looking woman, he thought. There was more to it than that. Part of it was that she was so damned smart. Samson worried that she might be even smarter than he was, which meant that she'd be too smart ever to think about hooking up with a man like him. If she really knew him, that is. Samson had been mighty careful so far to make sure that she didn't.

Her store smelled of molasses, leather, and pickles. It was stocked with all the things that a pilgrim might need; not just the staples like flour and sugar, but even wagon wheels and canvas. She made a good profit on everything, Samson knew, but the money didn't mean much to him.

He watched as Kate took a payment from some pilgrim and told him a little about what he might have to face on down the trail. Luckily for him the Indians weren't causing any trouble at the moment, but that could change overnight. Samson didn't have any problems with them, even living off where he did. They were afraid of him, and not just because of his size. They knew he didn't give a damn about whether he lived or died.

That was changing, though, now that he'd met Kate. He might have to consider moving closer to the fort if the Indians started giving him trouble. He shook his head. He'd never do that, and Kate most likely would never live where he did. He didn't know why he was wasting his time with silly thoughts about her.

He started to follow the pilgrim out of the store, stooping down and half turning sideways because he couldn't get his huge frame through the doorway otherwise.

"Why, Mr. Coleman," Kate said. "Are you about to go away without so much as a by-your-leave?"

Samson pulled back from the doorway and straightened up. He removed the battered hat that sat atop the mass of hair that hung down well below his shoulders.

"No, ma'am."

As much as Samson liked Kate, and as much as he would like to get to know her better, he nevertheless found it hard to talk to her. It was as if his tongue was paralyzed when he was around her.

"You're a liar, Mr. Coleman, and the truth's not in you."

Samson started to lie again, but he saw that Kate was smiling. He said, "Yes, ma'am."

"You could always buy something. I've been known to be friendly to a paying customer."

Samson knew she was joking, but he'd been intending to buy something anyway. "I could use some coffee if you have any."

"As it so happens, I do. And how much would you be wanting?"

Because Kate had initiated the conversation, Samson found it easier to talk to her than he usually did, and when she turned the conversation in an unexpected direction, he answered with more frankness than he'd meant to.

"Don't you get awful lonesome, living so far away from the fort?" Kate said as she fetched the coffee.

"I got my daughters to keep me company."

"And I'm sure they make wonderful companions. What I meant was, don't you ever miss talking to someone who's not part of the family?"

"You mean like you?"

She turned her face away, and Samson wondered if she hadn't blushed. But she turned back quickly and said, "I'll have you know I meant nothing of the sort. I was merely curious."

"I can see why you'd say that, and I'm sorry if I offended. Nobody wants to be around a rough old cob like me."

Kate handed him the coffee. "Don't you go running yourself down, Mr. Coleman. You're a good deal smoother than you're letting on."

Samson was uncomfortable with the direction the talk was going, so he paid for his coffee and took his leave. The interior of the store had been cool, as was the spring day outside, but Samson found that he was sweating. He knew that was a bad sign. He couldn't let himself go soft on a woman.

Not now; not when things were going just the way he'd planned them.

He told himself that he'd stop thinking about Kate Follett and turned in the direction of the Red Dog Saloon.

Fargo had no trouble finding a place at the table near Faith Coleman. True, he didn't get a chair, but he was able to find standing room nearby.

She was even prettier close-up than she'd appeared from across the room, he decided, and she seemed to enjoy the attention of the men, each one of whom tried to tell a better story than the one before. She laughed at their poor attempts at humor, she seemed impressed when they bragged about their hunting prowess or their ability with a rifle, and she looked sad when they told her the tales of their failures.

If she'd been a whore, Fargo thought, she'd be a rich woman in no time, but as far as he could tell from what he'd heard and seen so far, she had no ambitions in that direction.

At the moment, a man was telling her a tall tale about how he'd faced down two men who'd waylaid him outside a mining town in California.

"They planned to kill me right there," he

said. "There was a creek not far away, and they were gonna slit me open and fill my belly with rocks. Sink me in the creek so I'd never be seen again."

"Why would they do that?" Faith asked, wide-eyed, as if she'd never heard anything so frightening and exciting at the same time.

"Because I had my poke with me, and I had a nugget in it big as a pigeon's egg."

The other men around the table rolled their eyes, and those standing nudged one another, but Faith didn't seem to notice.

"But you're still here. How did you ever escape?"

"Well, now, that's a right interesting story," the man said. "You see —"

His voice died as the bat-wing door was pushed open and Samson Coleman came inside.

There was a sudden scraping of chair legs on the saloon floor as men pushed away from the table. The men who had been standing all around Fargo, elbow to elbow, scattered themselves around the big room so quickly it was hard for the eye to follow them.

The only one besides Fargo who didn't seem nervous was Faith. She looked toward the door and said, "Hello, Father. Is it time to go home?"

"Yes it is, daughter. I hope nobody here has bothered you in any way."

As he spoke, he stared around, letting his look rest on each man.

No one met his black gaze. Instead they looked at the floor, not that Fargo much blamed them. Samson Coleman was about as big a man as Fargo had ever seen, more than a head taller than Fargo himself and as massive through the body as that grizzly bear Cobb had spoken of not long before. He was as shaggy as a bear, too. The hair on his head looked as if it hadn't been cut in many years, and his thick beard, black with plenty of gray mixed in, hadn't been trimmed since his last haircut.

He stopped looking around when he came to Fargo.

The Trailsman wasn't like the others in the saloon. He wasn't intimidated by any man, not even one as big as Coleman. Their eyes locked for a few seconds, and then Coleman said, "Come along, daughter."

His eyes never left Fargo as Faith rose from her chair. She looked at Fargo, too.

"I don't believe I know you," she said when she walked by him.

"Name's Fargo," he said, touching the brim of his hat. "Pleased to meet you."

"Perhaps I'll see you again."

"I surely do hope so," Fargo said.

Faith walked by him and joined her father.

"Did you get what you needed at the store?" she asked.

Fargo could have sworn there was a double meaning in her comment, but the innocence of her face made him doubt it. And if there was, Coleman ignored it. He waited until she had walked past him, then gave Fargo one more stern look and followed her out the door.

"You're lucky he didn't mash you flat and then scrub the floor with you, Fargo," Cobb called from the bar when the pair had left.

"Why would he want to do a thing like that?" the Trailsman said.

Cobb crossed the room to stand beside Fargo. "Just to teach you a lesson. He could see the way you were lookin' at Faith, and you can bet he don't like that one damn bit. And you didn't back down none when he gave you the glare. He don't like that, either."

Fargo thought about the way the men had scattered away from Faith when Coleman had entered. He figured that none of them had tried anything fancy with her.

"Then why does he let her come here?" Fargo asked.

"I got no idea. He does, though, and we're

all mighty glad of it. Right boys?"

Those who heard him nodded their agreement, or said something in a low voice as if they were afraid that Samson might hear them.

"She sure does brighten up the place," Cobb said. "Makes a man forget his troubles better'n a good drink of whiskey."

He made a good point, and Fargo agreed with him. He couldn't help wondering why a woman like Faith would hang around a place like the Red Dog, however. She didn't seem to fit in, but there had to be a reason for it. It might be a good idea to find out what that reason was.

5

Another thing that Fargo had been wondering about was why Ferriday had hired him in the first place. He'd considered it more than once during his travel to Fort Laramie. Ferriday's passengers were being robbed, but not of much money. Even if Ferriday lost all his passenger trade because of the robberies, he'd still have his mail contract, and that's where the biggest part of his profits was made. The more he thought about it, the more convinced Fargo became that Ferriday hadn't told him the whole story.

Fargo wondered if it was just a coincidence that the robberies Ferriday seemed worried about had started around the time Samson and his daughters had showed up in the neighborhood. Nothing he'd heard so far threw any suspicion on them, but Fargo thought it would be a good idea to find out a little more about all of them if he could.

He thought he'd pay a visit to Kate Follett's store and see what she had to say.

Fargo wasn't the only one who was wondering about things.

"Who was that fella in the saloon?" Samson asked Faith as they walked to their wagon.

"Which one?" Faith said, though she knew very well who he was talking about. "There were a lot of fellas in the saloon today."

Coleman cut his eyes at her. "The big one wearing buckskins. I never saw him before."

Faith tried not to grin. "I didn't notice him."

"Don't give me that, girl. You spoke to him, and I saw you do it. You may be all grown-up, but I'm still your daddy. You tell me what you know."

Faith laughed. "All I found out was that his name is Fargo. He's a good-looking man, though, isn't he?"

Samson grumbled something about not knowing anything about men's looks and said, "I don't want him to interfere with our plans."

Faith laughed. "He won't interfere. Why should he?"

"I don't know, but I don't like the look of him."

"That's because he's not afraid of you."

"You noticed that, did you? Well, if he's not, he should be." Samson shook his head and changed the subject. "Did you find out anything else today?"

"Yes, I did," Faith said. "I'll tell you when we're on the way home."

"Is it something I'll want to hear?"

"I'm sure it is."

"Good," Samson said. "But I've changed my mind about going home. I want you to talk to that big fella some more before we leave."

"His name is Fargo."

"So you said. But we need to know more about him than that. I think I've heard that name before. He might cause us some trouble."

"Where did you hear his name?"

"I don't remember. That's why you need to find out more about him."

"It will seem odd if I go back into the saloon now."

"You won't have to," Samson said. "Look."

Faith followed his gaze and saw Fargo leaving the saloon. She also noted the direction he was headed.

"I think he's going to beat your time with Kate," she said.

"He better not try it. You head him off. You know what to do."

Faith knew, all right. Her father had trained her well. "Where will you be?"

"Since he won't be at the store, I'll go back there. I'll tell Kate I forgot something or other."

"I'll meet you there," Faith said. "I won't be long."

"He might not be as easy as you think."

"He's a man," Faith said.

Samson grinned. "He is, at that."

Fargo glanced over his shoulder and was surprised to see Faith walking in his direction, but he didn't object to the sight. He stopped and waited for her to catch up with him.

"Hello again, Mr. Fargo," she said when she reached his side.

She was tall and slender and looked nothing at all like her father. Fargo could see why Cobb was amazed that Samson had a daughter like her, and he wondered about the sisters. If they were prettier than Faith, they would sure enough be something to see.

"Just plain Fargo," he said.

"Very well. My name is Faith."

"So I heard. You have a lot of friends in

the Red Dog."

She smiled at him. "I make friends easily. I'd like to be your friend, too."

Fargo said that sounded like a fine idea. "I'd be happy to treat you to a drink," he added.

"I don't want to get to know you with so many other people around. Why don't we go somewhere that there's no one to bother us."

Fargo thought that sounded like another fine idea. "Where would that be?" he asked.

"I have a friend who lets me use her room now and then," Faith said. "Come along."

She walked a little ahead of Fargo and kept up a brisk pace as she led him toward the other large saloon near the fort. This one was the Palace, and it was bigger than the Red Dog for one main reason: it had more whores. It was off-limits to the soldiers, but that didn't keep them from going there.

Faith didn't go in the front but instead led Fargo around to the back, where Fargo saw a double privy and a pile of garbage, the smell of which assaulted his nostrils. Faith ignored it and went up to the door. She entered without knocking, and Fargo followed her into a hallway with doors on both sides.

"They're usually not busy in the afternoon," Faith said. "They're probably all out in the saloon, but I'll make sure."

She knocked on one of the doors, and when there was no answer, she opened it and looked inside.

"No one here," she said.

She went in and held the door open. Fargo entered, and she pushed the door closed.

The room wasn't much, but it had everything a soiled dove needed, including a bed with a faded blue counterpane, a washstand with a pitcher, bowl, and lamp on top, and a chair. A faint musky smell hovered in the air.

"You come here a lot?" Fargo said.

"No. Just when I want privacy."

"Whose room is it?"

"She calls herself Big Head Sue, but her real name is something different."

"I don't think I know her."

"I wouldn't expect you to. I met her when I was in the saloon one time, and we got to be friends."

She sat on the edge of the bed and patted a spot beside her. Fargo sat down.

"You spend a lot of time in saloons," he said.

"There's not much place else to go around Fort Laramie."

"The men seem to like you."

"They do, but they don't bother me. They're afraid of my father."

Fargo thought they had good reason to be, and he wondered why a man who was so protective of his daughter would allow her to sit in a bedroom with a man and not a sign of a chaperone within miles, unless you counted the whore to whom the room belonged, and she didn't seem to be anywhere nearby.

"But you didn't seem afraid," Faith continued.

"I was, though," Fargo said. "Didn't you see me shaking?"

Faith put a hand on his knee and leaned into his arm. "You're funning me now."

Fargo could feel the softness of her breast, and her red hair tickled the side of his face.

"I wouldn't lie to you," he lied.

"Then you're the only man I ever met who wouldn't. What makes you different, Fargo?"

"Maybe I'm not."

She drew away from him but kept her hand on his knee. He could feel its warmth through the buckskin.

"What are you doing in Fort Laramie?" she said. "You don't look like the other men I've met here."

"I've done some scouting for the army now and then," Fargo said, which was the truth even if it didn't answer her question. If she wanted to think it was an answer, that was all right with him.

"Then you know Colonel Alexander."

Fargo said that he did. He wasn't surprised that Faith did. He'd have bet she knew several of the officers, and maybe a few of the enlisted men.

"How long will you be staying?" she asked.

"I couldn't say. I do things besides scouting. Some other job might come along."

"And if it does, you'll just pick up and leave?"

"That's what I do. People call me the Trailsman. I guide wagon trains, take people where they want to go, do a little scouting — whatever comes to hand."

"Don't you ever think about settling down?"

Fargo didn't see any need to go into the details of his life. He had his own reasons for staying on the move. He'd spent pretty much all his life on the trail after the death of his parents when he was just a kid.

"The idea of settling down never entered my head," he told her.

"Not even if you found the right woman?"

Fargo didn't have to ask what she meant

by that, since she turned to him and looked into his lake blue eyes with her own. So instead of saying anything, he kissed her.

She responded without hesitation, opening her mouth, her tongue seeking his. Fargo fell back on the bed, pulling her along with him. Her soft breasts pushed into his chest, and he could feel his manhood rising.

Faith must have felt it as well. She pulled away from him and stood up.

"I'll make sure I fastened the door," she said.

When she'd done that, she turned to face Fargo and shucked out of her clothes so fast it was like a cardsharp's trick. Her body was very white, and there were freckles on her creamy breasts. The hair at the juncture of her legs was as fiery as that on her head.

Fargo got out of his own clothes almost as fast as Faith, and when she got a look at him, she gasped.

"You're much of a man," she said. She walked across the room and encircled his shaft with her hand. "Very much of a man."

She stepped closer and rubbed the tip of it against the wiry hairs on her mound. "Mmm. I knew I liked you from the minute you walked in the saloon."

Fargo pulled her to him, and they kissed again. He knew somewhere in the back of his mind that she was using him, and that she hoped to find out more about him when she'd weakened him down. Well, she was welcome to try. He'd figure out why later. For now, he was just going to enjoy it.

Faith broke off the kiss and lay down on the bed. "Do you know what to do with that big old thing?" she asked.

Fargo pretended ignorance. "I'm not sure."

"Well, come here and let me show you."

She spread her legs, knees up, and Fargo knelt on the bed between them.

"Come a little closer," she said.

Fargo inched forward until the tip of his tool was once again touching her pubic hair.

"A little bit more," she said, and the tip touched the magic button.

"Ahhhhh. Stay just like that for a second."

Fargo didn't move, but Faith did. She took hold of him and rubbed him against her while her hips wiggled on the bed. Fargo caressed the rock-hard tips of her breasts and she moaned. Her breath came faster, in short gasps.

"Now, Fargo," she said, and she guided him into her steaming slot.

He slipped easily inside. Already excited, he tried not to move too fast, but Faith urged him on with her twisting hips and tiny cries. Her head thrashed from side to side, whipping her red hair across her face.

Fargo moved along with her, no longer trying to keep it slow. She gripped him with her legs and pulled him deeply into her, holding him there while she spasmed again and again.

"Ahhh! Ahhh! Ahhh!" she cried, and then Fargo streamed into her like a geyser.

"Ohhhhhhh," she said, and it was almost a sob. She released him from her grip and lay limply.

Fargo rolled over beside her. They lay like that for a few minutes. After a while, Faith stirred, and Fargo thought she might be ready for another round.

That wasn't what she had in mind, however.

"My father's going to kill you," she said.

6

Women had said a lot of things to Fargo after lovemaking, but never that.

"Why would he want to kill me?" Fargo said.

"Because I'm not supposed to be here doing what we're doing."

Fargo ran a finger over the tip of one of her breasts. She shivered.

"I don't plan to tell him," he said. "What about you?"

"No, but he has a way of knowing."

"What did he think we were going to do? Sit in a parlor and chat? Just what were you supposed to be doing with me, anyway?"

Faith got up and started to pull on her clothes. "What do you mean by that?" she asked.

Fargo thought he might as well tell her the truth. "I saw the two of you watching me. I know he sent you to talk to me."

"He did nothing of the kind. He said he

wanted to visit with Kate over at her store, and I thought I'd just talk to you until he got back."

Fargo didn't believe a word of it. "Well, any time you'd like to . . . talk some more, I'm ready."

Faith buttoned her shirt. "I don't think I want to talk to you anymore. Good-bye."

She unfastened the door and left, not giving Fargo a backward look.

Fargo got his makin's from his shirt pocket and rolled a smoke with steady fingers. He lit the cigarette with a lucifer, and lay back to smoke and to think over what had just happened. He was sure Faith had intended to get information from him, but she'd gotten nothing at all. Could it be that she'd been so carried away by their lovemaking that she forgot what her real duty was?

On the other hand, he hadn't found out much about her, either. He blew smoke at the ceiling. The question was, why were Faith and her father so interested in him? It had to be more than just simple curiosity about a stranger in the area, Fargo thought, and that meant that they might be connected with the robberies.

He couldn't figure the connection, however. Faith might be dangerous in bed, but he had a hard time thinking of her as being involved in a stagecoach robbery.

Fargo sat up and looked around for somewhere to stub out the cigarette other than on the floor. He saw nothing, so he opened the window and tossed the butt outside. Then he stretched and got dressed.

Samson Coleman was upset with his daughter, although he didn't say so. He sat and smoldered in silence as the wagon bounced along, taking them to their cabin.

It was getting late in the afternoon, and the day was turning cooler. The wagon rattled along beside the river, headed for the mountains beyond the fort.

After they'd gone about a mile, Samson finally spoke.

"What I don't understand," he said, "is how you could *talk* to him for so long and not find out anything."

Faith looked over at the river. She didn't want to face her father. "I tried. He's not very talkative."

"It's a good thing I went to see Kate again, then. She knows him."

That got Faith's attention. "She does? What did she tell you?"

"That he's called the Trailsman. Works as a scout and guide. Sometimes for the army,

sometimes not. He's known to be a dangerous man if you cross him."

Faith had forgotten that Fargo had told
her his occupation. She was embarrassed to
realize that she didn't even care, not after
the way he'd made her feel. She'd had men
before, but never one quite like Fargo.

"Do you plan to cross him?" she asked.

Samson laughed. "You think I wouldn't?
He might be dangerous to some men, but
not to me. I'm not scared of him or any
man."

Faith didn't doubt him. She'd never seen
him back down from anything, which, come
to think of it, was one of his problems. The
main one, in fact, but she didn't want to
think about that right now.

"Could he be here because of us?" she
asked.

Samson considered it. "I don't see how.
Judging from what Kate told me, that
wouldn't be his kind of work."

"I hope it's not," Faith said.

"Why? If it was, would that worry you?"

"He's not like most men."

"You've changed your tune," Samson said.

Faith didn't answer for a few seconds.
Finally she said, "Yes, I have. There's more
to Fargo than I thought."

"I won't ask you how you found that out."

"Just as well," Faith said, sure that he already knew. "I wouldn't tell you."

Samson looked at his daughter, but she was staring at the river.

"You might as well tell me what you found out in the Red Dog, then. What plans do we need to make?"

"Can't I just wait and tell everybody at once?"

"Might as well," Samson said. "Be easier that way."

He clucked to the mule, and the wagon moved a little faster. Samson was ready to get home.

Kate Follett smiled when Fargo came into her store.

"Good afternoon, Trailsman," she said. "Where've you been keeping yourself?"

"Here and there," Fargo said. "Like always."

"You're like the wind, never in the same place. What brings you to Laramie?"

"Just looking for a job," Fargo said. He trusted Kate, but he wasn't going to let anyone know his real purpose. "You heard of any pilgrims needing a guide?"

"Not lately, but there's always a few coming along, thinking they can make it to Oregon all by themselves. By the time they get here, they mostly know better. You wait a few days, and you'll find somebody."

"Lots of new people here already. I met one named Samson today. You know him?"

"I know him. He's a strange kind of man, but a good one, I think. Deep down."

Fargo wondered how deep she meant. It must be a mighty long way. But if a woman was interested in a man, she could sometimes see the good in him that escaped a normal gaze.

"You like him," Fargo said.

Kate busied herself behind the counter and didn't look at Fargo.

"I guess I do. He comes by to talk. He's alone and needs company."

"Alone? What about his daughters?"

"That's not the kind of company I mean."

Fargo figured that if she was thinking that Samson could be tamed down to become a storekeeper if he had a woman like her, she was following a cold trail. He wasn't going to tell Kate that, however.

"Well," he said, "I wouldn't be surprised if he found the kind of company he was looking for before long. Maybe right around here." He looked around the store and settled down on a nail keg. "Been any excitement around here since the last time I came through?"

"Not unless you count stage robberies," Kate said. "With the Indians being quiet lately, that's about all the excitement we've had, and that hasn't been close to the fort."

Fargo had noticed several Indians outside the store. He said, "You been giving handouts again?"

"Now and then," Kate said. "Some of those people need all the help they can get. They're being driven off their land, Fargo."

The Trailsman held up a hand. "I wasn't criticizing. Just asking. Tell me about those robberies."

"There's not a lot to tell. The stage gets stopped, the passengers get robbed. Nobody's hurt."

"Not unless you count losing money as being hurt."

"I mean nobody's roughed up. This is a polite bunch of robbers."

"I guess that's why the colonel hasn't tried too hard to put a stop to them."

"If you've talked to him, you know that he's sent out some patrols. Nothing happened. It was just a waste of time, and he needs the men here."

"You say the robberies don't happen around the fort. Do they all happen in the same spot?"

"Not from what I've heard. The robbers

are too careful for that. They pick different places nearly every time."

Fargo didn't want to seem too interested in the robberies, so he picked a new topic. "Your friend Samson has some daughters, I'm told."

Kate gave the Trailsman a speculative look. "Knowing you, Fargo, I'd say you've already found out about those daughters."

Fargo grinned. "A little. Not as much as I'd like to know."

"You just keep away from them. They're fine young women, and they need someone who's willing to settle. They're all mighty pretty, and they'll find themselves fine husbands one of these days."

Fargo said he didn't doubt it. "But it's going to be slim pickings around the fort, unless they're looking to marry soldiers."

Kate nodded. "A soldier's wife has a hard time of it when he's stationed in a place like this. I think they're planning to do better."

"Won't be easy. Maybe they're planning to move on."

Kate told him she didn't think so, not for a while.

"It must get as lonesome for them as it does for Samson," Fargo said.

"They have plenty of company. They visit the fort often enough."

"I hear they spend a good bit of time in the saloons."

"Skye Fargo, don't you go talking about those girls any such way. I'll have you know they're fine young women."

Fargo thought he knew them better than Kate did, or at least he knew one of them better. He couldn't speak for the others.

A man came into the store about that time, looking for some harness leather. Fargo told Kate good-bye and left her to take care of the customer. It was time he talked to the stage agent.

7

Hal Calhoun was a short man who must have been somewhere around seventy. His bushy gray beard was stained with tobacco juice around his mouth. He wore an old black hat that looked as if a horse had stepped on it at one time and then tried to eat it. His tattered shirt was plaid flannel, his denim pants were dirty, and his boots had run-down heels.

"You the station agent?" Fargo asked him.

Calhoun shifted his chaw and said, "Who the hell wants to know?"

"I do."

"Mebbe so, but who the hell are you?"

"Skye Fargo."

Calhoun looked him over with a critical eye. "You're the one they call the Trailsman, ain't you."

"That's me."

"I've heard about you. Sorry if I seemed a mite unhospitable there. No offense."

"None taken. Ferriday should have sent you word I was coming."

Calhoun turned his head and spit a stream of amber-colored juice, then wiped his mouth on his shirtsleeve.

"Yeah, he did. Why don't we go inside and have us a talk."

The inside of the station wasn't much to see. There were a few cots, a cookstove, and a rickety table with four chairs. It was clean, however.

"I know it ain't much," Calhoun said. "Ferriday spends more on his horse feed than he does on his hired help. A fella like me ain't gonna find him a much better job, though." Calhoun dug around in his mouth with a forefinger, brought out a well-chewed hunk of tobacco, and tossed it in a bucket by the door. "Ferriday says you're gonna look into the robberies we been havin'. Said for me to keep my mouth shut about it, so I ain't told a solitary soul."

"I'll take your word for that," Fargo said.

"Damn right, you'll take my word for it. You ask anybody around this fort, and they'll tell you that if Hal Calhoun gives you his word, it's good as gold." Calhoun hooked one of the chairs with his foot and pulled it away from the table. He turned and straddled it, his arms resting on the back. "Now tell me what you want. I got work to do."

Fargo sat in another of the chairs and asked Calhoun to tell him what he knew about the robberies.

"Not very damn much. What you want me to tell you? Stage goes out, it gets robbed. Not a hell of a lot to say other than that."

"You must've talked to the drivers. You know what happens. I need some details."

"Usually it's an ambush, set up in some unlikely place or other along the road. The robbers'll drag a limb across the road, or roll down a rock, or just line up in the way so the stage can't go on. They make all the passengers get out, rob 'em, and ride off. All very polite, like they was in a drawin' room."

"And nobody gets hurt."

"Not yet. The passengers ain't real happy about it, even at that."

"Where do the passengers come from?"

"All over the place. Some of 'em come from Missouri, some of 'em come from right here. Not so many from here, though."

"Do the stage passengers have much of a layover here?"

"Long enough for me to cook 'em some grub." Calhoun motioned to the cots. "Long enough for some of 'em to sleep a while if they can. Most of 'em can't. When they lay down, they still feel like they're bouncin' up and down in that stage. Takes a while to get used to solid ground again."

"Any of them ever go to the saloons?"

"Some. If they got the time and the money."

Fargo thought that over for a minute. "Anybody ever get a good look at the robbers?"

"They've counted 'em. There's four. All of 'em with their faces covered with their kerchiefs and wearin' long coats. Not much to look at when you get right down to it."

"How do they sound?"

"Like robbers. What'd you think?"

"I think people have different kinds of voices," Fargo said, though he suspected Calhoun had known what he meant and was just being contrary.

"Well, I don't have any idea what kind of voices they got. Ain't nobody ever said. I get the idea they don't talk much."

"Ferriday says they never seem to get a lot of money."

"Hell, any money's a lot of money out here, Fargo. You ought to know that by now. There's Indians at the fort'd slit your gizzle for the money to buy a drink of whiskey."

"The robbers aren't Indians, though."

"Not that anybody knows of. Don't matter. Plenty of white men that'd kill you for the same money and the same reason."

Fargo nodded, acknowledging the truth of it. "When's the next stage coming through?"

"Tomorrow, 'bout noon," Calhoun said. "You can bunk here tonight if you've a mind to. I'll rustle us up something to eat. Won't be much."

"Sounds good to me," Fargo said, "no matter what it is. I'll fetch my horse and stable him here if that's all right."

"Mr. Ferriday's note said for me to give you whatever you wanted. I expect that means oats and water for your horse if you want 'em."

"Fair enough." Fargo stood up. "I'll be back in an hour or so."

"Take your time," Calhoun said. "I ain't in no rush."

Fargo went to get the Ovaro. He wondered about what he'd heard from Calhoun, and he wondered what Faith Coleman was doing about now.

The wagon carrying Faith and Samson rolled to a stop in front of a cabin well hidden from the trail. It was back among the trees along the river, and anyone not knowing it was there would pass it by without ever having had a glimpse of it.

A young woman not much older than Faith was drawing water at a well near the cabin. Her hair was not as red as Faith's, being more of a strawberry blonde, but the resemblance between the two was so striking that they might well have been twins.

When the wagon stopped, two more women came out of the cabin. One had dark brown hair, and the other was a pure blonde. They too bore a strong family resemblance to Faith. Not one of the four looked at all like Samson.

Faith stepped down from the wagon, and Samson drove it around behind the cabin to unhitch the mule.

"What did you find out at the fort?" the blonde asked. She was taller than Faith, with a slightly fuller figure. "Will we be riding again?"

"You're always in a rush to hear things, Hope," Faith said. "I'll tell you when Father is ready."

"You haven't told him yet?"

"Nothing. But we'll be riding out tomorrow, I can tell you that much."

"Damn," said the brunette, whose name was Charity. "I was hoping you wouldn't hear anything this time."

A woman named Prudence came up to them, carrying a bucket of well water. "If you'll move out of the door," she said, "I'll take this inside."

The other women moved out of the way. Prudence went past them without asking what they'd been discussing. She was the youngest, and of them all she had the least curiosity.

Her sisters followed her inside. The cabin had one large common room with a stove, table, and chairs. At the rear doors led to a small bedroom where Samson slept and a larger one for the sisters. There was a loft with a bed for visitors, but it was never used. The Colemans never had visitors. They didn't want them.

Prudence set the bucket of water down by a large wooden washtub. Her sisters gathered around the table, and Prue joined them while Faith shared the latest gossip from the fort. She offered nothing much to get their attention, until she mentioned Fargo. Hope and Charity stirred around and started to ask questions. Prue didn't appear to have any interest in the conversation even then.

"How big was he?" asked Hope.

Faith grinned. "Big enough. Bigger than I expected."

"You mean you've already . . ."

"Of course she has," Charity said. "You know Faith well enough to know that."

Faith looked offended. "You're just jealous."

"Maybe I am," Charity admitted, running a hand through her dark hair. "You always seem to have more luck with men than the rest of us when you go to the fort."

Prue seemed to pay no attention to the talk. It was as if she weren't even hearing it, but she was. She heard other sounds as well.

"You'd better hush," she said. "Father's coming in."

The others hadn't heard him, but Prue was right. Almost as soon as she stopped speaking, he stepped into the doorway, filling it with his huge frame.

He looked around the room for a second or two, then walked to the table and took the remaining chair, one that was larger than the others and reinforced so that it wouldn't collapse beneath him.

"Now, Faith," he said, when he was seated. "I'm ready for you to tell me about tomorrow's stage and what kind of passengers it'll be hauling. I hope it's good news."

"It's good enough," Faith said. "I met one man today who'll be taking the stage. He was headed west, but his horse broke a leg when it stepped in a hole about five miles from the fort. He had to walk in, and he said he'd decided to ride the stage to Fort Bridger before he bought another horse."

"What makes you think he has a lot of money?" Hope asked.

"I didn't say he had a lot, but he has enough to buy a horse at Bridger, where horses don't come cheap. He's wearing good clothes, and he bought a few rounds for the house while he was in the saloon. I think he has more money than just enough for the horse."

Samson nodded. "Faith's never been wrong when it comes to judging a man's holdings." He paused. "What about this Fargo fella? He look like he's got money?"

Faith looked at her sisters, all of whom managed to look serious and inquisitive, as if they hadn't heard anything about Fargo before.

"I don't think he's got much money at all," Faith said.

"What's he doing here, then?" Samson asked.

"He's just looking for a job."

"You right sure about that?"

"That's what he told me. We don't have to worry about him."

Samson didn't respond for a minute or so. Then he said, "I reckon you're right." He looked around the table at his daughters. "Well, if there's a man with money and we don't have to worry about anything, the four of you'll be riding out tomorrow. Are you ready to rob the stage again?"

"Why not?" Faith said. "We've been doing it long enough to know how."

"It's getting more dangerous, though," Charity said. "Sooner or later, we're going to get caught."

"It's bad luck to talk like that," Samson said. "You're not gonna get caught. Not as long as you can find out every time Alexander plans to send out a patrol. You've never had any trouble from him, and this time won't be any different from the others."

"I hope not," Faith said. "I don't think I'd like being in prison."

Samson gave her a black look, and Faith was sorry she'd mentioned prison. It wasn't a subject that they talked about much these days, though they'd heard plenty about it at one time in the past.

"You'll never go to prison," Samson said. "No daughter of mine will ever have to suffer that. I promise you."

Faith wondered how he could make a

promise like that. And she worried even though he had.

8

Calhoun provided a supper of biscuits and beans. The biscuits were burned on the bottom and a little bit too salty, but Fargo didn't complain. He tried to find out more about the robberies while they ate, but Calhoun didn't have any more to say about them.

"You might want to watch yourself if you're thinking about ridin' on the stage," the stage agent said, wiping a bean out of his beard with his fingers. He rubbed his fingers on one leg of his dirty pants. "You don't look like the usual kind of passenger, and those robbers'll know something funny's goin' on when they see you."

"I won't be riding the stage," Fargo said. He washed down a bite of biscuit with the bitter black coffee that Calhoun had brewed for them. "I don't plan on letting the robbers know I'm around."

"What're you plannin' to do then?"

Fargo had thought about it, and he'd decided that the best course of action would be to ride out along the stage route, maybe a little ahead of or a little behind the stage. There wasn't much place to hide on some stretches of the road, which would make it tricky. He'd have to be careful not to get spotted. On the other hand, the lack of cover would make things just as difficult for the robbers. They'd have to pick a spot with adequate concealment.

Fargo told Calhoun his plan, and the stage agent said, "When're you plannin' on goin' out, then?"

"Tomorrow seems like as good a time to start as any," Fargo said, and asked him to describe all the locations where the stage had been robbed in the past.

Calhoun named them off and observed that just about every possible place along the trail had been used for an ambush at one time or another.

" 'Fore long," Calhoun said, "those robbers'll have to start all over again and use the same places they started with, 'less they want to move on farther down the road, find 'em some new stage to rob or go into some other business. If you don't catch 'em, that is."

"There's something I've been wondering

about," Fargo said, pushing his empty tin plate away from him. "Where do the robbers come from? They must have a place to hide out around here somewhere."

"Plenty of places they could do that," Calhoun said, looking at the plate. "How'd you like those biscuits?"

"Melted in my mouth."

"Yeah, I just bet they did. Anyway, Colonel Alexander's had a look around for a hideout and never found a sign of one."

"What about people who live around these parts? Does Alexander trust all of them?"

"Not too many folks livin' around the fort that the colonel doesn't know. They may not be the cream of society, but he knows they didn't do any robbin'. Far as the ones livin' off from the fort a ways, well, they're all kinds. Most of 'em are old trappers who can't give it up, even now. They ain't robbers. And then there's Samson and his daughters. Can't figger that buncha girls of Samson's for robbers, can you?"

"What do you know about them?" Fargo asked.

Calhoun gave him a wicked grin. "The daughters, or Samson?"

"All of them."

"Don't know much. Don't know where they come from or where they were before they got here. They showed up here a while back, and they live in a house out off the trail somewhere. Haven't been there myself, though. That's just what I've heard. Don't know exactly where it might be. Folks seem to like the family, 'specially those girls."

"Did they come here before or after the robberies started?"

"Damn, Fargo, if you're not a suspicious fella. Samson, he might be a robber, all right. He looks mean enough, but there's just one of him. And those girls? I ain't seen the robbers, mind you, but I ain't never heard of four pretty girls who could pull jobs like that."

He stopped and thought about what he'd said, as if something had occurred to him for the first time.

"On the other hand, there's four of them and four of the robbers."

"And when did they get here?"

"It was a good while before the robbin' started. But I don't care about that. Don't you go gettin' any ideas about those girls, Fargo. You'd be dead wrong if you blamed them for anything."

Fargo wasn't so sure. Samson and his daughters had moved into the area near the fort before the time the robberies started. The four daughters spent a lot of time in the saloons, and there was nowhere better to pick up information than a saloon. If a passenger was leaving from the fort, they'd know about it, and they'd probably know how much money he was carrying if the other girls were as friendly and talkative as Faith. Besides that, they'd be able to find out when Colonel Alexander was planning to send a patrol along with the stage.

Calhoun was right in that it was hard to believe four women would be robbing the passengers in a coach, but Fargo had encountered plenty of strange things in his time. And he'd learned that a woman could do just about anything she set her mind to. Not many of them turned to robbery, but that was no reason to rule out the possibility.

Calhoun pushed back from the table and stood up.

"You gonna sit there all night moonin'," he said, "or are you gonna help me clean up?"

Fargo stopped thinking about the robberies and got busy.

The next morning Calhoun fried some ham and served it with the leftover biscuits. By this time they were more like rocks than biscuits, Fargo thought, but he still didn't complain. He had a feeling that made Calhoun feel worse than if he'd insulted him.

After they'd eaten, Fargo helped Calhoun clean up again. When that was done, he sat back down at the table and cleaned his pistol.

"You really think you're gonna need that thing?" Calhoun said.

"You never know," Fargo told him. "Might come in handy."

He finished cleaning the gun, then went to the stable to help Calhoun get the fresh horses ready for the stage.

"Got to change 'em pretty often," Calhoun said. "They get mighty tired pullin' that heavy coach. Drivers take it easy on 'em if they can, but it's still a strain."

When they were done, they went back to the agency building and found that the passengers had arrived. There were two of them, both men that Fargo had seen in the saloon the day before. They introduced themselves as Tom Anderson and William Allen. Neither one looked especially prosperous to Fargo, but when Allen said that he was going to Fort Bridger to buy a horse, the Trailsman knew he had some money on him. Anderson kept quiet about his plans.

Calhoun took their payment for the stage ride and pointed out a piece of paper that was nailed to the wall.

"You might've ridden a coach before," he said, "but in case you ain't, you oughta take a look at that. You might see something there that will help you."

Fargo had read the notice earlier. It told the passengers how to make their journey easier by doing a few simple things. One suggestion was for them to sit in the seat nearest the driver with their backs to the driver because that seat wasn't as bumpy as the rear seat.

"You can take a chaw," Calhoun said as the two men read the notice. "You can smoke if you want to, but it might make you sick. That coach will be rockin' something fierce."

"I've ridden a stage before," Allen said. "I know what to expect."

"I haven't," Anderson said.

"Be a bumpy ride," Calhoun told him. "Lots of swayin' and rockin', like I said. You'll get used to it."

"This says I shouldn't jump out of the coach if the horses run away," Anderson said.

"Sure enough," Calhoun said. "You'll be fine in the coach, 'less it turns over, which it ain't likely to do."

That wasn't exactly true, Fargo thought,

but he didn't think this was the time to argue the point. Anderson already looked as if he might back out of the trip.

"Anyway," Calhoun went on, "if you jump, you'll get hurt for sure. Bust your head open on a rock, or break your legs or arms. Horses won't run away anyhow, so don't worry about it."

Anderson didn't look convinced, but he said nothing. He and Allen sat at the table to wait for the coach, and Allen pulled out a deck of greasy cards.

"Care to play a hand, fellas?" he said, fanning the cards on the table.

Anderson said he was game, but Fargo and Calhoun declined. Calhoun had to start cooking up a meal for the passengers, and Fargo wanted to be outside to greet the stage when it arrived. He hoped to talk to the guard out of the hearing of the passengers, so he sat on an overturned nail barrel and waited.

It wasn't long before the coach rolled up in a cloud of dust. Fargo waited until the passengers, two men, got out and walked unsteadily into the station. The driver stood beside the stage and fanned himself with his hat. The guard stood beside him, and Fargo went over.

Both men were sun-browned, and their

skin looked leather-tough.

"I work for Ferriday," Fargo said, after he'd told them his name.

"I'm Prentiss," the driver said. "This here's Oliver. We've heard of you."

Oliver nodded. "Ferriday gave all the drivers and guards the word about you."

"Where's Calhoun?" Prentiss said.

"I'm right here, Prentiss," Calhoun said, coming outside. "Give me a little time to see to the passengers before you get in a hurry to change teams."

Fargo took Oliver aside while Calhoun and Prentiss unhitched the horses.

"Have you ever been robbed?" Fargo asked.

"You mean on this route? Yeah, a couple of times. I'm pretty new on the run. Prentiss has been stopped four or five times, I think."

"Tell me what happened when you were there."

"There was four of them," Oliver said, confirming the other accounts Fargo had heard. "Came on us just as we were rounding a bend between a couple of big rocks. Fired some shots in the air, nearly spooked the horses, but Prentiss kept 'em steady. He stopped the coach, and they said for me to get the passengers out, so I got down and did that. Two of 'em sat on their horses with their rifles pointed at us while the other two took the passengers' money and watches and things. When they was satisfied, they mounted up, and all four of 'em rode away. I got the passengers back on board and we went on our way. That's about all there was to it."

"What did they sound like?"

"Who?"

"The robbers."

"They had their faces covered, so it was hard to tell much about how they sounded." Oliver thought it over. "Now that you mention it, though, I guess it was only one of 'em that had anything to say the whole time. The leader I guess it was."

"Were they short? Tall?"

"Kind of middlin', I reckon. I wasn't really noticin' that kind of thing. I had my eye on the rifles, mostly."

Oliver wasn't much more help than anyone else had been, Fargo thought.

"I'm going to ride along behind you today," Fargo said. "Out of sight of the trail. If anything happens, I'll be around somewhere."

"That's all right with me, but don't come chargin' up and get me or the passengers shot. Mr. Ferriday wouldn't like that." He motioned to the Greener he'd left propped in the boot. "Don't get yourself shot, either."

"I'll be careful," Fargo said.

"And don't go talkin' about any robberies in front of the passengers," Oliver added. "It gets 'em nervous and scared, and there's no tellin' what they might do if the robbers show up. Maybe something stupid, and I don't want that to happen. I don't want anybody gettin' killed. 'Specially me."

"Nobody's going to get killed," Fargo said.

He hoped he wasn't wrong about that.

9

The Coleman sisters kept their horses in a corral well away from the house. A visitor to the house, assuming they ever had one, would never know about the horses. The sisters walked to the corral dressed in their long coats. Their hair was tucked up under their hats, and their neck scarves were ready to pull up over their faces.

Samson walked along with them, giving them the usual instructions. He thought it was important to repeat them every time the girls went out, though he suspected that his daughters didn't bother to listen anymore.

"Don't worry about a strongbox," he said. "The line hardly ever carries any valuables. Just take whatever the passengers have."

"We know," Charity said.

"And do what you have to do. If someone tries to pull a gun, you shoot him before he does. You hear that, Faith? Prue?"

"We hear you," Faith said. "We know what to do."

"Well, I just want to be sure. Nobody's gotten feisty with you yet, so you might get careless."

"We won't get careless," she assured him.

"I hope not. And don't talk any more than you have to. We don't want anybody to get the idea that you're women. Charity's the one with the deepest voice. Let her do all the talking for you."

Nobody said anything. They'd heard it all before. Several times before.

"Nobody's gonna follow you after you leave the coach," Samson went on. "That is, nobody's gonna follow you if Faith is right and Alexander's keeping the troops around the fort."

"I'm right," Faith said.

"I don't doubt it," Samson said. "She's always been right in the past. So you come straight back here, understand?"

Charity sighed. "We understand."

"You're good girls," Samson said. "Doing what your old father asks."

"We know your reasons."

Samson's face darkened. "That's enough about that. I don't like to talk about it."

They came to the clearing where the corral was located, and the girls got their saddles from a little tack room that Samson had built. When they'd saddled up, Charity said, "We'll see you soon, Father."

Samson watched them as they rode away, looking as innocent as four women dressed like bandits could. They do their daddy proud, he thought.

Fargo watched as the four passengers got on the stage. The two who'd arrived at the station on the coach still looked a little shaky, even after their meal and whatever rest they'd managed to get. Allen looked resigned, and Anderson seemed a bit apprehensive. If he'd never ridden in a coach before, Fargo thought, he had reason for his painful expectations.

The fresh team was hitched up, and Oliver was already up on his perch. The driver climbed up, said a few words to Calhoun that Fargo didn't catch, and then the coach was rolling away.

"How long a lead you plan to give 'em?" Calhoun asked as he and Fargo stood watching the stage disappear in the distance.

"Not long. I'll go saddle my horse."

Calhoun took off his battered hat and slapped at his pants to knock some of the trail dust out of it. When he had put it back on his head, he said, "When do you reckon you'll be back?"

"That depends on what I run into," Fargo said.

"Not much of anything, I'm thinkin'."

Fargo turned and started for the stable. "You're probably right."

Calhoun walked along beside him. "Could be I'm wrong. What then?"

"Have to wait and see."

"Supposin' you run into more than you can handle. Get shot up, mebbe killed."

Fargo grinned. "You're a real cheerful fella, Calhoun. Make a man feel good about what he's doing."

"Hell, I don't mean to say anything's gonna happen to you. Don't think it will. I was just sayin' what if."

"You just let Ferriday know. Tell him to send more men next time. Ten or twenty at the least."

They reached the stable with its smell of manure and hay. Calhoun watched while Fargo saddled the Ovaro. As he tightened the cinch, the Trailsman said, "Saying that I don't get killed or shot up, what's for supper?"

"Biscuits and beans," Calhoun said. "Might throw in some bacon if I'm feelin' good."

"I could use some bacon."

"Didn't say bacon. Said I'd throw some in the beans. If I felt like it."

"Just as long as you have the biscuits," Fargo said.

The Coleman sisters set up their ambush at a slight bend in the road where a couple of large rocks concealed them and their horses.

"I don't like this place," Faith said. "I don't think the driver will slow down enough for us to stop him."

She didn't think the rocks were big enough to hide them well, either, but she didn't mention that.

Charity, who had picked the spot, said, "It's as good as any other place we've used. We won't have any trouble."

Hope looked skeptical. Prue just looked away, as if she didn't care one way or the other, and Faith thought that she probably didn't. Prue didn't seem to care much about anything as far as Faith could tell.

And that was bothersome. People who didn't care were the ones who made mistakes. Faith trusted Charity and Hope to do the right things at the right time, but she wasn't ever sure what Prue might do. She wondered if the others felt the way she did, but she knew this wasn't the time to ask.

"I hope you're right," Faith told Charity.

"It won't be easy to stop the coach if the driver goes right on by us."

"He'll slow down. Besides, we can't go back to any of the other spots where we've stopped the coach before. They'll be watching for us."

"They might be more likely to be watching where they *haven't* seen us before," Hope said.

"Next time, you can pick the place," Charity said.

Faith laughed at the show of temper. "This is no time for us to be fighting. We'll stay right here and see what happens. The coach should be along in half an hour or so if it's on time. How do you plan for us to stop it?"

"The driver will slow down," Charity said with confidence, as if that argument had been settled. "When he does, we'll ride out behind the coach and fire a few shots into the air. That should be enough to stop him."

Faith didn't think so. She had a bad feeling about the whole enterprise, for reasons she couldn't quite put into words. She'd never felt this way before a robbery, not even her first one. She didn't like it.

"Now that we're away from Father," Hope said to her, "tell us a little bit more about this Fargo that you . . . met at the fort."

Faith said there wasn't really much more to tell, but Charity and Hope said they knew better. They wanted to hear everything. Faith was about to give in and tell them when Prue said, "The coach is coming."

Faith had often thought that Prue's hearing was preternaturally acute. She always heard things before any of her sisters did.

"Are you sure?" Charity said.

Prue just nodded.

"She's never wrong," Hope said. "We'd better get ourselves ready."

They covered their faces up to the eyes with their bandannas and checked their weapons. By the time they'd finished those small preparations, they could all hear the rumbling of the wheels.

"As soon as he passes by us, we'll go after him," Charity said. "If he's going slowly enough, we can ride right alongside."

"And get shot by the guard," Faith said.

"He's not going to shoot us. He doesn't want to start a fight that might get the passengers hurt."

The bad feeling Faith had wouldn't go away. Her sister's words just increased her unease. She was about to say something more, but by then the coach was at the rocks. It was going too fast, Faith thought, but it was far too late to do anything about

91

that now.

Prentiss and Oliver weren't expecting anything at the gentle curve. There wasn't much concealment, and it just didn't seem like a good spot for the ambush.

They were both relaxed, Oliver with his shotgun in the crook of his arm and Prentiss leaning a little forward on the seat, peering ahead through the light dust stirred up by the horses' hooves.

Prentiss hardly slowed at all for the curve as the road bent around the rocks. It wasn't sharp enough to worry about, and he wanted to keep up a good pace.

"Damn," Charity said, as the coach went past. Her voice was muffled, but the sisters heard her well enough. "Let's get after him."

They kneed their mounts, and the horses charged out from the cover of the rocks, but the stage was already well past them by the time they got onto the road. They started after it, firing their pistols into the air.

Faith saw the guard look back over the top of the coach at them. It was almost as if he were looking right into her eyes. The scattergun he held wasn't a threat at that distance, but he looked as if he might use it if they got within range.

She would have told her sisters to give up

the chase if they could have heard her, but with the firing pistols and the pounding hoofs, that wasn't possible.

The driver urged his horses on, as if he had something personal at stake. Maybe he was tired of being robbed. Faith wouldn't blame him if that was the case.

He might as well get used to it, however, Faith thought. The Coleman gang wasn't going to give up.

Not now.

Not ever.

10

Fargo heard the shots and got the Ovaro moving. He hadn't really thought he'd run into a robbery on his first day on the job, but it seemed like luck was with him. If you could call a robbery lucky.

He wasn't far away from the fracas, and he thought he could catch up easily when the coach stopped. Then he'd see what he could do about bringing an end to the robberies.

"You better slow down and pull up," Oliver yelled to Prentiss. "They're just gonna chase us till the horses drop, theirs or ours."

Prentiss knew Oliver was right, but it galled him to think that he was about to be robbed again. He was getting damn sick and tired of it. Still, there was no use killing the horses or maybe turning over the coach and getting a passenger hurt or worse. He hauled back on the reins.

Charity saw the coach slow and smiled with relief under her scarf. For a while she'd been worried that she'd made a mistake this time, and Father wasn't the kind to forgive an offense easily. She glanced around to be sure that her sisters saw what she did, and all of them met her eyes briefly. They knew what to do from this point on without any telling.

They caught up with the coach. Charity and Hope holstered their pistols and pulled their rifles from the scabbards. They held them steady, and Charity, deepening her voice, told Oliver to put down his shotgun.

The guard did as he was told, putting the gun in the boot out of sight. He didn't look happy about doing it.

Charity ignored him and the driver and rode over to kick on the door of the stage with the toe of her boot.

"Everybody out," she said.

The men inside got out and stood beside the coach. One of them looked as if he might collapse, but the other three seemed calm enough.

Faith and Prue dismounted. Faith put her pistol away and pulled a cloth bag from her shirt. Prue kept her pistol at the ready while Faith opened the bag and held it out to the men.

"Give him your money and valuables," Charity said, keeping her voice as deep as she could.

The men complied, except for Allen. He said, "I don't have anything to give you."

Faith knew he was lying. She looked back at Charity. The other three men hadn't produced much, just watches and a few coins, and that wouldn't satisfy Samson. Allen was the only one who was actually carrying some money.

"We don't want to have to shoot you," Charity said to him, catching Faith's look, "but we'll do it if you don't fork over your money."

At Charity's words, Faith cocked her pistol. The click of the hammer so frightened Anderson that the two on either side of him had to hold him up.

"Well?" Charity said.

For a second it looked as if Allen wouldn't give in, but then he sighed and reached into a pocket.

He pulled out a derringer, and Prue shot him.

The sound of the shot was more than Anderson could stand. He fainted, and the two men beside him no longer tried to hold him up. He fell to the ground on his side and lay there, one foot twitching.

Allen stumbled back against the coach. Prue's bullet had grazed the upper part of his arm, and blood stained his jacket. The derringer lay on the ground where he had dropped it. Prue kicked it under the coach.

"Put your money in the bag," Charity said, and this time Allen did as he was told, using his left hand to get it out of a pocket concealed in his jacket.

Faith closed the bag and tied it. She and Prue got back on their horses and waited.

"Get back on the coach," Charity said to Allen. "That's just a scratch. You'll be all right."

Allen used his good arm to pull himself back inside, and the two men who were standing by the fallen Anderson turned to follow him.

"Not you two," Charity said. "Pick that man up and help him."

The two men grabbed Anderson under his arms and jerked him to his feet. Between the two of them they lifted him up and shoved him into the coach. He was coming to by then, and he managed to get himself into his seat. The two men followed him on board.

"You can get on your way now," Charity said.

"We got a wounded man in there," the

driver said.

"He's fine. His friends can put a patch on him. Get on out of here."

The driver picked up the reins, flapped them, and the coach moved slowly away. It began to gain speed, and the sisters sat on their horses until it was almost out of sight.

"Time for us to move," Charity said.

After the robbers moved off after the stagecoach, Fargo rode to the rocks and stopped there to watch the proceedings. Having been assured that the robbers never killed anyone, he didn't see the need to intervene. His plan was simple. He'd let them finish their business, and then he'd track them back to their hideout. They wouldn't be expecting that, and they'd probably make it easy for him. He didn't know what he'd do after they reached their destination, but the best thing might be to go back to the fort, give Colonel Alexander the location, and let him take over.

When the shot rang out and Allen staggered backward, Fargo thought at first he was going to have to break cover. Anderson fell, too, but Fargo saw that Allen was the one who'd been shot, and that he was only wounded.

Anderson, however, seemed to be worse

off than Allen, lying there facedown in the dust, but Fargo was sure that Anderson hadn't been shot. He was the nervous type, and Fargo figured correctly that the shot had just scared him unconscious.

Things moved swiftly after that, and after the robbers had done what they set out to do, the coach faded into the distance with the four robbers watching it go. After a while, they turned from the trail and rode away.

Fargo stayed behind the rocks until they too had disappeared from sight. Then he went after them.

Faith couldn't understand why she was still worried. There was no reason why she should be. Everything had gone well except for Prue's having shot one of the passengers, and he hadn't been badly hurt.

Faith had been shocked when Prue fired the shot, but as usual Prue was a little bit ahead of everyone else. It wasn't just her hearing that was especially acute. She'd known that the man was pulling a pistol before any of the other sisters, almost as soon as the man himself had known. But now she seemed to have forgotten the whole thing.

Faith didn't understand Prue at all, but

she'd proved that, in this case at least, her apparent lack of concern for her surroundings wasn't dangerous to her sisters, though it might be dangerous to anyone else who happened to be around.

Prue rode a little ahead and a little apart from the others as they headed home, as she always did. She was one of them, but not deeply connected with any of them.

Hope and Charity rode side by side, smiling and talking, but Prue ignored them.

Faith just wished that the bad feeling she had would go away. She rode up beside Hope and Charity and told them that she was still worried about something, though she couldn't say what it was.

"You should be happy," Charity said. "We have the money, Father will be pleased, and the stage is on its way with nobody the worse off."

"You forgot the man Prue shot."

"That was fast thinking on her part," Hope said. "Charity and I would have been too slow to save you. I hope you thanked Prue."

Faith hadn't done that, and she made a promise to herself that she would as soon as they got back to the cabin. Even that promise, however, didn't do anything to remove the uneasiness that overwhelmed her.

Every now and then Prue would look over her shoulder, but she wasn't looking at her sisters. She was surveying the countryside as if looking for something.

Or someone.

"There's nothing out there," Hope told her. "We haven't seen an Indian for weeks, and nobody's tracking us from the fort."

Prue turned around and rode on without replying. Hope looked at her sisters and shrugged as if to say, "That's just Prue's way."

It was, Faith knew it was, but the empty feeling in her stomach remained. The closer they got to the cabin, the more apprehensive she felt.

"I hope Father's all right," she said.

Charity gave her an incredulous stare. "Why wouldn't he be all right? If there's anyone in the world who has little to be afraid of, it's Father. He's bigger and stronger than anyone. He's had to be."

"So have we," Hope said. "Don't you think something could happen to us?"

"Of course. But not to Father."

Faith wished she shared Charity's confidence. As they approached the trees that surrounded the cabin, Charity took off her hat, allowing her dark hair to cascade down over her shoulders. That was all the signal

Samson would need to know that everything had gone more or less as planned.

Prue pulled back on the reins and stopped her horse. She sat still in the saddle as Charity and Hope rode past. Faith reined in beside her and asked why she'd stopped.

Prue shrugged. "Just a feeling I have."

Faith's stomach fluttered. "What kind of feeling?"

Prue didn't say anything.

"I've been worried all day," Faith told her. "I thought I'd feel better when we were home safely, but I don't."

Prue shrugged again and flicked the reins. She and Faith rode on to the cabin where their father was waiting for them.

11

The robbers had made no effort to hide their tracks, and Fargo had no difficulty following them. Colonel Alexander could have tracked them easily, or one of his scouts could have, had the effort been made. The robbers must have gotten overconfident because of their success.

For most of the way there was no means of concealment, so Fargo stayed well behind his quarry. He didn't need to keep them in sight, thanks to the plain trail they had left.

After a while he had a pretty good idea where they were headed. The river wasn't too far away, and they must have had a place to stay somewhere near it. When he saw the trees in the dim distance, he figured there was a cabin nearby, so he stopped the Ovaro. He'd wait until around sundown and go in when the shadows started falling in the trees, and he'd go in walking. That way he'd be less likely to be spotted if they'd posted a lookout. He didn't think they would, not as careless as they'd been about being followed.

He threw a leg over the saddle horn and got out his makin's to roll a smoke. He had a while to wait, but that didn't bother Fargo. He was good at waiting.

Faith was happy to be back in the cabin with her father and her sisters gathered around, and her mood lightened a little. She listened while Charity told Samson about the robbery, and he frowned only once, when told about Prue shooting the passenger.

"As long as he wasn't killed," Samson said. "The good book tells us, 'Thou shalt not kill.' "

Faith was pretty sure the good book had something to say about robbery and fornication, too, but Samson had never shown an inclination to disapprove of those. Oh, he didn't like to talk about how his girls went about getting information, because he was sure to know that sometimes they used more than honeyed words and sweet smiles. But as long as his grand scheme was carried out, he overlooked things like that. To him, Faith knew, the money didn't really matter. The aggravation and the inconvenience to the stage line did.

Besides, she knew that Samson's reason for not wanting them to kill anyone had nothing to do with the Bible. He was well aware that as soon as one of the passengers was killed, or the guard or driver for that matter, there would be serious consequences. They'd been left pretty much to do as they pleased so far, and that was fine, but there would be a big change if killing came into it.

When Charity finished telling the story and Samson had praised them for a job well done, the sisters got busy fixing supper. Or three of them did. Prudence had disappeared.

Fargo went in low and quiet, reaching the trees and fading silently into the shadows. He saw the cabin ahead, with lamplight already glowing in the windows.

While he waited, he'd thought about the situation. Four women robbing stagecoaches?

It didn't make any sense to Fargo. They weren't taking enough money to make it worthwhile. And Samson had to know about it. Why did he allow it? Didn't he know how dangerous it was? Even though no one had been killed so far, it could happen at any time. It could have happened today if the bullet one of the women fired had been a little farther to the left. If anybody got killed, there was going to be hell to pay.

For that matter, the women were in as much danger as the passengers and Ferriday's employees. If there was shooting, they were going to become instant targets. Why take the risks? What was the reason?

Fargo watched the shadows of insubstantial forms pass in front of the window. He couldn't tell how many people were in the room, but he figured there were five, Samson and his four daughters. The women hadn't spotted him and had no way of knowing they'd been followed.

He thought over his choices. He could go back to the fort and tell Alexander what he'd discovered, or he could go right up to the door and confront Samson and his daughters, asking them what the hell they thought they were doing.

There was nothing appealing about the second choice. It was too risky. He'd seen a man shot already, so he knew the women weren't gun-shy.

Fargo heard something behind him, not much more of a sound than a couple of feathers of a bird's wing might make if they brushed together, but that was enough to alert him.

He'd just started to turn when something exploded in his head and blackness engulfed him.

Fargo came to in a bed. It wasn't much of a bed. It had what seemed to be a corn-shuck mattress that whispered and rattled beneath him when he made any movement at all.

Not that he could move much more than his fingers and toes. He seemed to be paralyzed, and his head hurt as much as if he'd been kicked by a mule. Or a couple of mules.

His eyes were open, but he couldn't see a thing. Wherever he was, it was black as the bottom of a mine at midnight.

He blinked. No change. He blinked again and thought he could see a glimmer to his left. He couldn't turn, because of the pain in his head, but he cut his eyes that way. Yes, there was starlight, coming through a window.

That meant he was indoors, but that was all he knew. He tried to move again, and this time he managed a little bit of a wiggle. The corn shucks rustled, and his head felt like somebody had laid it open with a war ax.

"Be still," said a voice from the end of the bed. "You're not going anywhere."

The Trailsman recognized the voice. It belonged to Faith Coleman. He opened his mouth to answer, but his mouth was so dry that only a croak emerged.

"I'll get you a drink," Faith said, and Fargo heard a chair scrape on a wood floor.

A pitcher clinked on a cup, and Fargo tried to move again. He couldn't, but this time he knew what the problem was. It wasn't paralysis. He was tied to the bed.

Faith came to stand beside him. He couldn't see her well because of the darkness, but he could make out the vague outlines of her form. She bent over to lift his head with one hand and put the cup to his lips with the other.

When he raised his head, pain seared him down to his toes. He clamped his teeth together until it passed. After it did, he drank, but not too fast, trying not to dribble on himself.

He drained the cup. Faith took it away and sat back down in the chair where she'd been.

"What happened?" Fargo said.

"Prue hit you," Faith said.

"Prue?"

"Prudence. My sister."

"She must be strong."

"She's no stronger than the rest of us. She used her pistol butt on the side of your head, just behind your left ear. She didn't split it open, if you're worried about that."

Fargo was embarrassed. He'd let himself be caught by a woman. And hit in the head besides. The robbers weren't the only ones who'd gotten careless.

"Don't let it bother you," Faith said, as if she sensed his embarrassment. "Prue's not like other people. Nobody else would ever have known you were out there."

Fargo figured he'd have to take Faith's word for that, but it didn't make him feel any better about the way things had turned out.

"Why did she hit me?"

"You were snooping around. We Colemans don't like people who come snooping around, and she had a feeling you wouldn't behave yourself if she didn't put you out of commission." Faith paused. "What were you doing out there, Fargo?"

"I wasn't sneaking. Just scouting out the place. I told you scouting's what I did."

"You weren't even on your horse. I'd call that sneaking, I think."

"What about my horse?"

"You don't have to worry about him.

Hope went out and fetched him. He wasn't real friendly to her, but she brought him in."

"Thank her for me," Fargo said.

A small noise that might have been a laugh escaped Faith's lips.

"You're awfully polite for a man who's been hit in the head and tied to a bed."

"I like to make the best of things. How bad is my head?"

"Not as bad as it would be if Father had hit you. He's much stronger than we are. You'll be fine in a few hours, but you're going to have quite a knot where Prue hit you."

She wasn't a doctor, but Fargo figured she had it right. He'd been hit before and recovered soon enough.

"What happens to me now?" he said.

"That's up to Father. He's the one who makes the decisions around here."

"Where is he?"

"Sleeping. So are my sisters. I'm supposed to watch you until midnight. Then I'll wake up Prudence, and she'll take over."

Fargo wasn't sure he wanted to have any more to do with Prudence.

"You don't think I'm going to get away, do you? How likely is that, with me tied up like this and with my head feeling like I've been scalped?"

"Father says we're not taking any chances with you. You might as well lie still and try to sleep."

Fargo didn't think he'd have any trouble lying still. With the way he was tied, he didn't have much choice.

On the other hand, he didn't consider sleep a very likely possibility, not the way his head was throbbing. He was wrong, however. After a few seconds he closed his eyes and was almost immediately asleep.

Sometime later on he dreamed that he was being chased across the plains by four beautiful women, all of them naked. They didn't want loving, however. They all waved tomahawks and intended to scalp him as soon as they could catch him. The dream didn't last long, however, and after that he didn't dream anything at all.

12

When Fargo awoke again, a patch of gray sky was visible through the window. It wouldn't be long until the sun came up, he thought.

He lay quietly for a minute, then moved his head again to see if it was any better. It wasn't.

"Good morning, Mr. Fargo," someone said.

Fargo was getting tired of telling people not to call him *Mister,* but he did it anyway.

"Just Fargo. Which one are you?"

"I'm the one who hit you."

Fargo tried to remember what Faith had told him about which sister had sneaked up on him, but he couldn't, and he was afraid the blow to his head might have addled him.

"Prudence," the woman said, helping him out. "They call me Prue."

Fargo remembered then. He said, "How did you know I was out there?"

"I just know things sometimes. I don't know why. My sisters say it's my good hearing. Maybe it is."

Fargo wasn't sure good hearing explained it. He'd never had anybody sneak up on him like Prue had, not without giving some kind of sign.

"You hit me pretty hard."

"I'm sorry about that."

Her tone was the same as it had been when she'd given him her name. She didn't sound at all sorry to Fargo.

"I'm going to need to get up from here before long," he said.

"I don't think Father will allow that."

"A man who's been in a bed all night just naturally needs to take care of some things in the morning," Fargo said.

"There's a bucket here." The flat tone again. "Father will be along in a little while to help you. You'll just have to hold it until he gets here."

If there was one thing Fargo was sure of, it was that he didn't want any help in taking his morning piss.

"If you'll just untie these ropes, I'll take care of it all by myself."

"I can't do that. They're getting up now. Father will be here soon."

Fargo didn't know how she could tell that

the others were getting up. He couldn't hear them stirring.

And then he did, somewhere below where he lay. He'd always thought his hearing was as keen as anybody's, but Prue had heard them first. Or maybe not. Maybe she'd known somehow or other that they were about to wake up. Faith had said Prue wasn't like other people, and Fargo was starting to believe it.

"Are we in a loft?" Fargo said.

"That's right. There's a ladder nailed to the wall. I don't think you're in any condition to climb down, so it wouldn't do you any good if I untied you."

Fargo moved a leg that was starting to lose feeling, and the mattress rustled loudly.

"You just lie still," Prue said. "Everything's going to be fine."

She said that the way she said everything, as if she were about as concerned with Fargo's fate as she would have been with the fate of a buffalo chip. As far as Fargo could tell, she might even have cared more about the chip.

The noises down below were louder now, and Fargo heard the cabin door open and close a few times as people went outside to use the outhouse.

It was almost sunrise, and the light was

better now. Fargo could make out Prue's features. She had reddish hair and fair skin. Fargo couldn't guess at the color of her eyes, nor could he tell much about her figure. But her face showed a cold beauty that he could admire.

His mouth was dry as straw, and he told Prue that he could use a drink.

Prue fetched him a cup of water, but she wasn't as solicitous of his head as Faith had been. When she took away the cup, Fargo heard splashing down below.

"My sisters are bathing in the washtub," Prue said. "No use you trying to look. You couldn't see a thing from where you are."

For one of the few times in his life, Fargo wasn't interested in looking. The truth of it was that he was feeling sleepy again, and he knew that wasn't right.

He'd slept right through the night, and he should have been wide-awake and alert. He wasn't. He felt drowsy and logy. He worried that his brain had been jarred around in his skull. He knew that a good knock on the head could cause something like that.

He wondered if he'd get better, or worse, as the day went along. For that matter, maybe Samson wouldn't let him get any better. Maybe he'd just kill him outright.

Prue didn't say any more to Fargo, and

after a while the splashing around ended. Not long afterward, someone else climbed up into the loft.

"You can go down and take your bath now, Prue," she said.

When Prue had left, the woman looked Fargo over and said, "I'm Charity."

"I'm Fargo. Are you going to untie me?"

"No. I know you need some relief, and Father will be here soon."

Fargo had heard that one before, but he didn't comment.

The stove was lit below, and before long Fargo could smell coffee boiling.

"We'll have breakfast in a little while," Charity said. "Do you want coffee?"

Fargo thought about what the coffee might do to his already bloated bladder.

"I don't think so."

Charity laughed. She was a dark-haired beauty, with full lips and a warmly sensuous gaze, nothing at all like Prue's cold demeanor.

"I can understand why you might want to skip the coffee," she said.

She sat in the chair. "My sister says you're a very . . . big man. Is that true?"

"You can see me lying here."

"Maybe I can't see everything I want to see."

Fargo wished he weren't sleepy, and that he was thinking more clearly. He had a feeling that if he said the right thing, Charity would be glad to give him a lot of pleasure right there in the loft. If there was a right thing to say, however, it didn't come to him.

It was just as well, because in only a few seconds he heard the door open and close, and then the clear clanking of a chain.

"Father's on his way up," Charity said. She stood. "It was nice to meet you, Fargo."

"My pleasure," he said.

Samson's head appeared over the ledge of the loft, and then the rest of him heaved into Fargo's sight. Charity moved aside and let him get off the ladder. He had to crouch down to avoid knocking his head on the rafters. He had a length of chain wrapped around his right shoulder.

"You can go now," he told Charity, and she went down the ladder without another word.

Fargo watched her go. She was much more pleasant to look at then her father.

"You've met all my daughters but one now, Fargo," Samson said. His voice was a deep rumble. "What do you think of them?"

Fargo didn't want to say what he thought of the women, and he didn't like Samson's tone. Not that it mattered. He had other concerns.

"They're beautiful. I need to piss."

"We'll take care of that right now," Samson said.

He pulled the chair over to the bed and padlocked the chain around Fargo's right ankle. He tossed the other end over a rafter and padlocked the end to the chain. He gave it a yank and, when the rafter didn't budge, he seemed satisfied.

"I'm gonna untie you, Fargo. Then you can stand up and take that piss."

It didn't work out quite that way. Fargo found that he was so dizzy that he had to sit on the side of the bed for a few minutes before he could stand. It was a good thing he sat because his legs were so wooden that he couldn't have walked on them anyway. When the circulation returned, the legs tingled as if they'd been frozen and were now thawing out. It wasn't a pleasant sensation, but Fargo endured it without comment. It didn't bother him nearly as much as his head did.

When he was finally able to stand, feeling a little dizzy, Samson put the bucket in front of him.

"Have at it," he said, and Fargo did, filling the bucket with the sound of a rainstorm on a tin roof.

When he'd finished relieving himself, Fargo felt a little better, but the ache in his head hadn't gone away, nor had the dizziness. He sat back down on the side of the bed.

"What do you have in mind to do with me?" he said.

Samson shoved the bucket under the bed with his foot and sat in the chair. It creaked and groaned under his weight.

"I think I'm going to make you a stagecoach robber," he said.

"You can't make me do anything."

Fargo's voice had a lot more assurance than he actually felt. In his condition, he wasn't up to fighting against anything Samson proposed.

"Oh, I think I can make you," Samson said. "What with you tied to my chain like you are, I can make you do a lot of things. But that's not what I meant."

Fargo wished he could think more clearly. He put his hand to his head to rub it, but thought better of that idea.

"What the hell did you mean, then?"

"I meant you're going to take the blame for all the robberies around here. You and your gang."

"My gang?"

"The three men that've been helpin' you

rob those coaches," Samson said.

"I don't know what you're talking about."

"That's all right," Samson said. "I'm just about to explain it to you."

13

Before Samson told Fargo anything, Faith poked her head over the edge of the loft and handed Samson a cup of coffee. When he took it, she reached back down and came up with another cup for Fargo.

"Charity thought you might like to have this now, Fargo," she said.

Samson took the cup from her and handed it to Fargo, who discovered that he did indeed want it. As he sipped the hot liquid, he imagined his head was clearing a little. His stomach rumbled.

"Bring Fargo some corn bread," Samson said. "That's all we have," he added. "Corn bread and molasses."

It sounded good to Fargo. He had to be getting better, he told himself. Otherwise, he wouldn't be hungry.

Faith brought up the corn bread and molasses on a tin plate. There was no fork, but Fargo set his coffee cup on the floor and managed to eat just fine with the flat-bladed knife that was on the plate.

After he finished, he set the plate on the floor and picked up the cup. He drank the rest of his coffee, which was a lot better than he'd had on the trail to Fort Bridger. Then he looked at Samson.

"Well?" he said. "Didn't you have something you wanted to tell me?"

"I was gonna tell you how you're about to be a stagecoach robber. It's easy enough, and you don't have to do a thing. We'll do it for you. Charity'll be goin' to the fort today, and she'll have a talk with Colonel Alexander. She'll tell him that you and your gang rode by here and tried to rob us but that we holed up in the house and ran you off."

"The colonel won't believe a story like that," Fargo said, knowing better.

"You'd be surprised what a man will believe when one of my girls tells him. They can be mighty persuasive."

There wasn't any doubt about that, Fargo thought.

" 'Course that leaves me with a little problem," Samson continued.

Fargo had a feeling he knew what the problem was, but he didn't want to ask, and he didn't have to. Samson was happy to tell him.

"The problem's you," Samson said. "What I think I ought to do is open you up, fill you with rocks, and sink you in the river." He paused, looking regretful. "But I don't hold with killin'. The good book tells us it's wrong, and I go by that even if it would solve my problem."

"I think the good book has something to say about robbery, too," Fargo said.

Samson brushed that criticism aside. "Says an eye for an eye. I believe in that."

"You can't get every eye there is."

"What chapter of the good book is that from?"

"That's the book of Fargo, chapter two."

"Don't believe I've read that one. Don't matter, though. I'll take whatever revenge I can get."

"Why?" Fargo said. "Why put your daughters in danger? They're not getting enough to help you much, and sooner or later they'll be caught."

"Gonna be later, now that ever'body's lookin' for you as the ringleader of that treacherous gang of robbers that's been plaguing the stage line," Samson said with satisfaction. "As to why they're doing it, that's a long story."

Fargo kicked his leg to one side, rattling the chain.

"I have plenty of time," he said, "if you're not going to kill me."

"I'm not. Not right now, anyway. Just don't know yet what I'll do."

"Well, if you're not going to kill me, you can at least tell me what the hell's going on."

Samson got up and retrieved Fargo's plate and knife. He called down, and Faith climbed up the ladder to get them. When she was gone, Samson sat back down.

"In the first place, my daughters are doin' the robberies instead of me because I'm too hard to hide, even with my face covered."

Fargo nodded. Samson's size was enough to make him instantly recognizable, no matter how he tried to conceal his identity.

"And in the second place," Samson said, "it's their revenge as much as it is mine, and maybe more."

The ache in Fargo's head increased but his understanding didn't.

"Ferriday did something to them, did he?"

"Did it to me, to them, to my wife." Samson lowered his head. "The son of a bitch."

Samson sat with his head bowed for several minutes. While Fargo didn't think he was praying, he said nothing, waiting for Samson to continue.

Finally Samson looked up, but he wasn't

looking at Fargo. He wasn't looking at anything in the loft or even in the cabin. He had the appearance of a man staring beyond the walls, across miles, across years.

"It was down around Albuquerque," he said after a while. "I was a young man then, in the strength of my youth. Had me a mighty fine wife, four little girls, and a good life workin' a little mail run. Then Ferriday came along. He wanted the mail run, and offered to buy me out." He paused. "Well, I wasn't selling, and it turned out it didn't matter to Ferriday what he had to do to get it. If it meant getting rid of me then that's what he'd do. And he did."

Samson's voice trailed off. He sat quietly, shaking his head slowly.

"How did he get rid of you?" Fargo said.

"Had me put in jail. Said I stole from him, which I never did. He paid off the sheriff and the judge, not that it cost him much, and the next thing I knew, I was in the calaboose. Look to the left and see a wall, same on the right, and all around. Nothing but walls. But that wasn't the worst of it, no, sir. There was a copper mine down there, and the prisoners had to work the mines all day, down in that hellhole with so little light it might as well have been nighttime, and hard to breathe besides. Go down

125

before daylight and come out after dark to march to the jail. Years went by, and I never saw a blue sky."

Fargo had heard about the jail Samson was talking about. What the big man was saying was all true.

"That jail was hot in the summer and cold in the winter," Samson said. "Vermin of all kinds covered me up. We never got to take a bath, not even once while I was there. I got used to the smell, bad as it was. Hardly noticed it after a while. I never got used to the filth and the dirt, though, nor the rats and the bugs. That's why we wash up every day here. I don't ever want to be filthy again."

"I don't like being dirty, either," Fargo said, sensing an opening. "Maybe I could have a wash down there in that tub of water."

Samson almost smiled. "I don't think so, Fargo, not today. I got to decide what to do with you first."

"You don't want to treat me the way you were treated."

"No, nobody oughta be treated that way. It was like bein' in hell, Fargo, and that's God's own truth. I never heard a word about my wife and babies while I was in that place, not till I'd been there four years, and what I heard then like to have killed me."

He stopped talking again, as if the memory of what had happened to him and his family affected him now almost as much as the real event had.

"What I heard," he said, "was that my wife had died of a fever and that my girls were all alone. Word was that they were tryin' to raise themselves, but I knew that sooner or later someone would take 'em to raise, and let 'em forget all about me and Sarah. That was my wife's name, Sarah. Well, I couldn't have that, but I didn't see what I could do about it till one day a guard got careless when we were leavin' the mine. They put leg irons on us when we came out, one by one, two guards on one man, one with a gun and one to put on the irons. But the guard with the gun looked away before the other one got the irons on me. I kicked that one in the head and grabbed the gun from the other one. He took off at a run, and so did I, just in the other direction. I don't know how many prisoners they lost that night, but I was one of 'em."

"They must have come after you," Fargo said.

"If they did, I never knew it. There was too many of us runnin' loose for one man to worry 'em much. I went straight to my place, or what used to be my place. My girls were there; the littlest, that's Prue, not even five years old. Her sisters were tryin' their best, but the house was nearly as bad as the jail. Charity, she's the eldest, was just goin' on twelve. It would've been better if someone had taken 'em in, but I had 'em then, and we got out of there that very night, headed north. We've lived here and there ever since, with me waitin' for my chance to get that eye for an eye."

Fargo thought about the story and Ferriday. Ferriday was a man who'd come up a long way in life, and Fargo knew he'd gotten his start down in New Mexico. He knew that the mail run Ferriday had now wasn't the first one he'd owned and that Ferriday didn't plan for it to be the last.

What Fargo didn't know was how Ferriday had gotten his start and what kind of man that proved him to be. If Samson was telling the truth, Fargo regretted having taken on the job from Ferriday.

At the same time, the Trailsman knew that Samson was going down the wrong trail. He was endangering his daughters, and he wasn't accomplishing what he'd set out to do.

"You're not hurting Ferriday," Fargo said.

"You're just a pest that he wants to get rid of."

"If that's what I am, that's fine. I'm gettin' my revenge on him slow. My girls are gettin' theirs, too."

"You're going to get them killed or hurt. Dammit, Samson, you can't let them keep on with this. It's not right, and you know it."

Fargo didn't think he'd put his argument very forcefully, and he blamed his head. He had a feeling, however, that even if he'd been thinking more clearly, he still couldn't have talked any sense into Samson.

"You can't tell me how to live my life, Fargo. Can't anybody do that."

"What about Kate Follett? Does she know what you and your daughters are up to?"

"Now you look here, Fargo, don't you go bringin' Kate into this. She don't have a thing to do with it."

"I heard you were soft on her."

Samson stood up, almost bumping his head on the rafter above him.

"Where'd you hear that? Even if it's so, and I ain't sayin' it is, it's no business of yours. You better not mention her again, you hear me?"

"If you think you're going to marry her, you've got another think coming," Fargo said as if he hadn't heard. "She's not about to marry anybody involved with robbing stagecoaches."

Samson seemed to swell and expand to about twice his already impressive size. He leaned forward, reaching toward Fargo with his immense hands, and the Trailsman thought for a second that he might have gone a step or two too far.

And maybe he had. Samson looked as if he'd forgotten what the good book said about killing. But Fargo was saved from having Samson snatch his head off and throw it out the window by a call from below.

"Father! I'm ready to leave. Are you going with me?"

Fargo recognized Charity's voice, and the call was enough to get Samson's attention. He stood still for a moment, his hands dangling at his sides, breathing heavily and noisily through his nose.

"You better get a hold on that temper of yours," Fargo told him. "It's going to get you in trouble one of these days."

"More like it's gonna get *you* in trouble if you don't watch what you say." Samson paused to draw in some deep breaths, getting control of himself. "I'll be going to the fort with Charity. You can sit here and think about things. Don't try to get away. I still haven't decided what to do with you, and I might decide that the good book don't forbid me to kill you after all."

Fargo said he didn't think he could just sit there all day. It wasn't natural.

"You don't have a choice," Samson said. "But I'll see if I can find you something to do. We have a book somewhere. You can read that."

"What book?"

"Something about a pathfinder. That ought to be just the thing."

Fargo wasn't so sure.

14

Samson and Charity had been gone for about an hour before Hope came into the loft. She had a thick book that she set in the chair.

"Father said you might enjoy reading something," she said. "We don't have a lot of books. Just this one and the Bible, and that's all."

"The one about the pathfinder," Fargo said, standing up to greet her.

"That's the one. It's about a man who —"

"Never mind telling me," Fargo said. "I don't think I'd like it."

"We've all read it several times," Hope said. "It being the only one we have."

Fargo sat on the bed. "Don't forget that Bible."

"That's Father's favorite. He reads that one, and we read this one."

Now that he could see her, Fargo realized that Hope was at least as beautiful as her sisters, maybe even more beautiful. Her blond hair shone in the light from the window, and she wore a man's shirt tucked into denim britches in a way that revealed pleasing curves. For that matter, the britches were tight enough to make things even more interesting.

Fargo's head was better, but it still hurt. His thinking was still a little muzzy, too, but he knew well enough that he wasn't up to reading. He sat back on the bed, and then lay down.

"Are you still feeling poorly?" Hope said.

"I've been better."

"I have an idea about something that might help."

She walked to the edge of the loft and looked down. "Prue, why don't you and Faith take a walk along the river. Or it might be a good idea to keep a lookout down the trail."

"Nobody's going to come looking for me yet," Fargo said.

"Maybe not, but you never can tell," Hope said.

"Are you sure you don't need us in here?" Faith said from below in a teasing voice.

"I think I can . . . handle everything just fine," Hope said.

"All right then," Faith answered. "Come

along, Prue. It's a nice day for a stroll."

"I don't want to stroll," Prue said.

"Never mind that. You come with me."

Fargo heard the scuff of feet, and the opening and closing of the cabin door. Hope started to remove her shirt.

For the first time in his life, the Trailsman wasn't sure he was ready for what was about to happen. His head was still sore, and the dizziness hadn't left him.

But when Hope had the shirt off and when Fargo saw the perfect globes of her breasts with their large brown nipples, he knew that he'd be up to the task. In fact, he was already getting up to it, as the bulge in his pants attested.

Hope smiled down at him. "I can see that you're interested in the cure I have for you."

She slipped out of her pants and kicked them aside. The blonde hair at the V of her crotch was so lightcolored as to be almost invisible.

The bulge in Fargo's britches got even larger.

"You'd better shuck those things before you break through," Hope said, and Fargo didn't waste any time doing so. He couldn't get rid of his pants because of the chain, but he pushed them down to his ankles.

When he was as naked as he was going to

get, Hope looked him up and down, smiling in admiration.

"Faith sure wasn't lying about you, Fargo. You have what it takes. It's a shame you're chained to the bed."

"I can walk a little way," he said, and to prove it he moved toward her, hobbled only a little bit by the chain and his britches.

Hope didn't wait for him. She met him halfway, and they pressed their bodies together. Fargo felt the urgent heat in her as she ground her mound against his thigh.

Fargo bent and kissed her, and her mouth opened, hot and slick. Her tongue sought his, and for a while they stood there with Fargo aware of a number of sensations: the heat and stiffness of her nipples; the firmness of her breasts; the stiffness of his rod as it stood at attention between them, burning against her skin.

She pulled away a half step and reached down for him, running her long white fingers lightly over the tumid tip of his shaft.

"You're a sick man," she said. "I think you need to lie down."

Fargo thought that was a good idea. He was a little dizzy, and he didn't think the chain would allow for his usual spirited performance. So he lay on his back on the bed to see what Hope had in mind for him.

She knelt beside him and took his shaft in her hand. At first she rubbed it slowly, lingering at the tip, and then she sped up. Soon her hand was flying, and Fargo felt the tension building behind his knees. He closed his eyes and reached toward her breasts. When he felt the stiff nipple of one of them, he gave it a feathery touch.

Hope stopped pumping him. Fargo felt her hair tickling his belly, and he opened his eyes just in time to see her engulf him with her hot, greedy mouth. He felt her tongue working on him, and she moved slowly up and down. As she inhaled more and more of his length, she began to make a low humming sound in her throat.

Fargo stiffened all over as every feeling in his body concentrated in one particularly sensitive spot. He was about to spasm uncontrollably, but Hope removed her mouth just in time to prevent it.

"I think you're about ready for the real thing," she said, smiling. "I know I am."

She stood up and straddled him on the bed, lowering herself onto him. She was so slick and ready that Fargo slipped right in, his rod plunging into the hot grotto right up to the curly pubic hairs.

Hope sighed and moved on him, raising and lowering herself calmly. Her eyes were shut tight, and her head was thrown back. Her lower lip was caught between her teeth, her hands on her hips. The shucks rustled beneath them like a cornfield in a windstorm.

Fargo put his hands on her breasts and cupped them so that the nipples burned into his palms.

Hope moved faster. Fargo had nearly reached his peak again, but she slowed down a bit to make things last as long as she could.

"This . . . is . . . so . . . good," she said.

Fargo would have agreed, but he wasn't talking. He was just enjoying the sensation. He'd forgotten all about the pain in his head and the dizziness.

Hope pressed herself down on him as far as she could before beginning to rotate her hips, rising as she did so. Soon she was moving so rapidly and in so many directions that Fargo was afraid she might fly off the handle, but she was too much in control for that.

"Now, Fargo!" she said. "Let me have it now! Now! Now!"

Fargo let her have it. He pumped into her and the hot stream shot out of him like a geyser.

When it was over, Hope collapsed atop

him for a few seconds. Then she raised herself off him and sat on the edge of the bed.

"I sure hope Father doesn't decide to kill you," she said. "It would be a terrible waste."

Fargo had to agree with her. He started to sit up but fell back on the bed. His head was spinning.

"Are you all right?" Hope said.

Fargo wasn't sure. He knew that he shouldn't have exerted himself, but he'd do it again if the same situation arose. Often the situation would arise again almost immediately, but Fargo knew there wasn't a chance of that this time.

"I haven't killed you, have I?" Hope said, a note of anxiety creeping into her voice.

"I don't think so," Fargo told her. "I'm not so sure about it right now, though."

Hope laughed. "If you can joke about it, you must be all right."

Fargo didn't really feel like joking. He just needed a little sleep, that was all, a little sleep and rest. He managed to pull his pants back up first. Then he closed his eyes and drifted off.

15

Samuel Dobkins looked nothing at all like the dude Fargo had met in Saint Jo not so long before. He wore dusty trail clothes, and his boots were covered with dust. Even his black mustache was dusty. He looked more like a prospector who'd spent a lot of time in the hills than a man who worked in an office with J. M. Ferriday.

He was also very disturbed by what he was hearing from Hal Calhoun, although he took great pains not to show it.

"Are you saying that Skye Fargo was the leader of the outlaw gang?"

"That's right," Calhoun told him. "I don't blame you for bein' surprised. I couldn't hardly believe it, myself. Don't seem possible that the Trailsman would have gone down the owlhoot trail."

It didn't seem possible to Dobkins, either, since he knew that Ferriday had sent Fargo to Fort Bridger only recently, whereas the robberies had been going on for some time. This wasn't what he and Ferriday had planned on, not at all, and that didn't please Dobkins a bit. He liked it much better when things went according to plan.

"Where did you hear this news?" he asked Calhoun.

"It's all over town. A fella told me earlier this mornin' when he come by to shoot the breeze."

They were in the way station, where Dobkins had just arrived on the stage. Dobkins had overheard Calhoun talking to the driver about the robberies and had joined the conversation. The driver had gone inside to eat and rest, and Calhoun had carried on the talk with Dobkins alone.

"You oughta be glad to hear it," Calhoun said. "I doubt those robbers'll hit the stage again now that they've been rousted, and now that we know who the leader is."

"But the Trailsman?" Dobkins shook his head in disbelief. "It just doesn't seem likely."

"Nope, it sure don't. He was just here yesterday, nosin' around and asking questions about the robberies. Now I can see that he wasn't being curious, though. He was hopin' to find out what we knew and maybe to find out what was on the stage. I guess anybody can use some extra money, even a fella like him. Anyway, like I said, you don't have to worry none about gettin' robbed today."

"I hope not," Dobkins said. "I'm not going any farther on the stage. I'm stopping here at Fort Laramie for a while, and I like to think I'll be safe."

"Well, I can't vouch for that. I can tell you, though, you'll be hearin' a lot more about the Trailsman if you stick around. Be a good story to tell your friends when you finally get where you're goin'."

Dobkins said he was sure that was true.

"Since you're stoppin' here at Laramie for a spell, I might's well introduce myself," the stage agent said. "Name's Hal Calhoun."

Dobkins shook Calhoun's rough hand. "I'm Larry Forbess," he said. "Pleased to meet you."

After he left the stage agent, Dobkins headed straight for the Red Dog Saloon in a hurry. He was supposed to meet someone there, and while it didn't matter if he was late, he wanted to find out more about Fargo as soon as possible.

Arriving at the saloon, he slapped a little of the trail dust from his clothes and hat, brushed some of the dust off his mustache, and went in.

For the middle of the day, the saloon was doing a booming trade, and Dobkins surmised it was because of a beautiful young woman sitting at a table with men buzzing around her like a swarm of bees.

The man Dobkins was looking for wasn't among the swarm. He sat alone at a table off to one side. He was compactly built and wore a clean shirt and a black hat. His sun-darkened face would have been handsome if not for the knife scar that started at the edge of one eye and ran all the way down to his chin.

Dobkins got a glass of beer at the bar and walked over to the table where the man sat.

"Hello, Fowler," he said.

Fowler tipped him the barest of nods.

"Mind if I sit?"

"That's what you came for, ain't it?" Fowler's voice was gravelly and low. "Go ahead."

Dobkins sat down and took a swallow of his beer. It was about as bad as he'd expected.

"You heard the news?" Fowler said.

Dobkins set his glass down on the table. "Yes. What in the hell is going on here?"

"Don't ask me. I just got in late yesterday. All I know is, some fella named Skye Fargo's been blamed for all the robberies. I hear he's been shot and wounded, shot and killed, or maybe just run off. Stories vary. I expect you know more than I do about it."

"We can't talk here," Dobkins said. The saloon was noisy, and they had kept their voices down, but Dobkins didn't want to take any chances. "Do you have a room?"

Fowler grimaced. "It ain't like there's any fancy hotels around here, Dobkins."

"You have to be staying somewhere."

"Yeah. There's some pilgrims let me sleep in their wagon last night. I figured I'd just make me a camp tonight and sleep there."

"Surely there's a saloon with rooms."

"If you want to pay through the nose for 'em. Mostly the rooms are for the whores."

"I have some money. Where do we go to get one of these rooms?"

"There's a place called the Palace." Fowler chuckled. "You ain't very likely to run into any kings and queens there, though."

"It'll do," Dobkins said. "Let's go."

He didn't even bother to finish his beer.

The room cost more than Dobkins wanted to pay, and it had clearly been used for fornication fairly recently. But it was the best thing available. He took a seat on the only chair, leaving Fowler to sit on the bed.

Fowler looked around as if hoping one of the room's previous occupants might show up and surprise him.

"All right," Dobkins said. "Tell me what's going on."

"Like I said, I just got here, same as you. You're the one with all the plans."

"The plans might not be worth a damn now, not with what's happened."

"Yeah. I don't see how Fargo can be a part of this, though. Didn't you hire him to investigate the robberies?"

"Ferriday did. You know the way we had it planned."

"Sure," Fowler said. "He comes out here, looks around, makes people suspicious, and gets killed during a robbery."

"That's close enough. It's going to be hard to finish the plan now that he's already been killed."

"He ain't been killed. That's just one story that's goin' around. I heard the straight of it, right from that black-haired gal in the saloon. It was her place that Fargo and the outlaws attacked. The family fought 'em off, and she says Fargo got away. He might be wounded, but accordin' to her he's not dead. Not yet, anyhow."

That news did nothing to cheer Dobkins up. The way he and Ferriday had planned things, the men sticking up the stagecoaches made the perfect scapegoats for the big robbery that Ferriday and Dobkins had planned themselves. But Ferriday needed more than scapegoats. He needed one particular person to be left for dead on the trail, while Ferriday's own men made off with the money. It wouldn't do for Fargo to be part of the actual outlaw band, and it wouldn't do for him to be dead, either.

The big robbery had been Ferriday's idea, but Dobkins had helped work out most of the details.

Ferriday needed money. The mail route was doing well, but not well enough to support Ferriday's extravagance. He liked to live high, and so did his wife, who liked expensive things imported from the East, even from Europe. Ferriday had built her a big new mansion that had to be furnished with only the best. He had enormous expenditures.

Ferriday also wanted to start another mail route to improve his financial situation, but the money wasn't available. Ferriday had to have money. He needed it quickly, and he didn't care how he got it, which was why he'd agreed to go against his usual policy of not carrying valuable shipments on his stagecoaches.

The Mercantile Bank of Saint Jo had approached him about a shipment of bullion to a sister bank in Oregon. Ferriday had agreed to haul it, with the thought of stealing it himself. It had been Dobkins' idea to put the blame on the outlaws who'd already been making a nuisance of themselves on a very small scale. Dobkins and Ferriday didn't want the outlaws to rob the stage with the bullion on it, however, and that was where Fargo came in.

"We can count on him showing up at the right time," Dobkins had told Ferriday. "We'll tip him that there's going to be a robbery, and then see to it that he's killed when he tries to break it up. The rest of the outlaws will 'escape,' which should be easy enough since they won't even be there."

Ferriday hadn't seen how it was possible for such a plan to work.

"The guard and the driver will know there wasn't a robbery," he had said. "They'll talk sooner or later unless we split with them, and there's not enough money for that."

Dobkins hadn't been worried. "We'll have our own guard on the stage."

Ferriday hadn't been sure they could subvert one of the guards, but that hadn't bothered Dobkins in the least.

"I know someone we can use. The regular

guard will never leave Fort Laramie. We can pay our man out of pocket change."

"What about the driver and the passengers?"

"Don't book any passengers on the run. The man I hire will take care of the driver."

That was all Ferriday had wanted to hear. The less he knew about that part of things, the better, and Dobkins had assured him that things would go smoothly.

Now, however, Fargo had messed them up somehow.

"We still goin' through with it?" Fowler asked, interrupting Dobkins' thoughts.

"Of course we are," Dobkins said. "We have to. Maybe it's best this way. Fargo's already taking the blame."

"Yeah, but that means he's not gonna ride up to the coach to stop a robbery and get shot."

That had been the plan. Fargo and the driver would be dead, and Fowler would be the only witness. The money would be gone, and the outlaws would take the blame. It had seemed simple enough when Dobkins was laying it out. Now, however, there wouldn't be a body.

"We'll think of something," Dobkins said.

"Yeah," Fowler said. "We'd better."

16

Samson should have been satisfied with the way things had worked out. At first, people found it hard to believe that Fargo was part of an outlaw gang, but by afternoon most of them had convinced themselves that they'd known it all along.

As one man put it, "We all wondered why he came snoopin' around here. Tryin' to find out how much people knew about the robberies, that's why. Wanted to be sure he was in the clear before they robbed another stage."

Unfortunately for Samson, however, one person who didn't believe a word of that kind of talk was Kate Follett.

She'd known Fargo for a long time, and she believed that he was honest down to the bedrock.

"There's not a finer man in the West," she told Samson. "I don't want to hear you say anything more against him, not in my store or anywhere else."

"But I saw him with the outlaws," Samson said.

"Did I just tell you not to say anything against him? You might have seen somebody who looked like Fargo, but it wasn't him. And don't you try to tell me that it was."

Samson had another problem as well. Colonel Alexander had been almost as hard to convince as Kate, even though Charity had ways of being convincing that weren't available to her father. Even though she used all her persuasive abilities, Alexander had never come all the way around to believing that Fargo was involved in the robbery.

"Fargo implied to me he was investigating the robberies," Alexander had said.

"That was his way of covering up," Charity explained, but she wasn't sure that Alexander had believed her.

So when Samson and Charity started for home, Samson was unable to content himself with the knowledge that most people believed the worst about Fargo. All he could do was worry about the ones who didn't believe it.

He'd have worried even more if he'd known what Fargo was up to at the cabin.

When Fargo woke up from his rest, he couldn't hear a sound in the place. Either all three sisters were sleeping, or they'd gone outside.

Fargo sat up. He didn't feel dizzy, and he found that his head didn't hurt. At least it didn't hurt as much as it had. Another good thing was that he was no longer drowsy. Even after a full night's sleep, he'd been drowsy earlier.

It also seemed to him that his mind was clear for the first time since he'd been hit. Maybe his brain hadn't been jiggled around too much after all.

If that was the case, then he had to start thinking about how he was going to get out of the cabin. He had a feeling that sooner or later Samson was going to overcome his scruples about killing, and if that happened Fargo would find himself lying at the bottom of the Laramie River with rocks for innards. He didn't think he'd like that at all.

He relieved himself in the bucket, noticing that someone had emptied it while he was asleep, for which he was grateful. He didn't much like the idea of sleeping over a bucket of piss.

When he was finished, he shook off the last drops and put his tool away. That done, he looked up at the rafter around which Samson had locked the chain. It was thick and heavy, and Fargo didn't think even Samson could break it, much less a man weakened by a knock on the head.

He looked down at his ankle. Samson had taken away his Colt and his Arkansas toothpick. Otherwise he could have cut off his leg and escaped that way.

Fargo shook his head. Gently. He still wasn't thinking straight if a crazy thought like that could enter his mind. There had to be a better and easier way to get out of the cabin and out of Samson's hands.

Just at that moment the door opened and the women came inside. Fargo could hear them chattering and laughing. He thought he heard his name spoken, but he wasn't sure. If they were talking about him, though, he didn't want to know what they were saying.

Before he could say anything to them, they started to shush each other, reminding themselves that Fargo was asleep. Faith's voice rose above the others.

"Hope really tired him out this morning. He's slept most of the day."

"I did no such thing," Hope said, laughing. "I don't have any idea what you're talking about."

Faith joined her sister's laughter. "You're a liar and the truth's not in you."

They started shushing each other again. Fargo wondered about the other sister who had been there earlier, Prue. He hadn't heard her voice at all.

"I'm awake," he said from the loft. "You don't have to be quiet."

He heard giggling, and then some discussion about who would get to go up and see about their unwilling guest. Faith won out, and soon her head poked up above the edge of the loft.

"How are you feeling, Fargo?" she said, climbing up to join him. "Better, now that you've had some rest, I hope."

Fargo ignored the sarcasm in the way she said *rest*. He asked where Prue was.

"She's down there with Hope. Prue doesn't talk much. Is there anything I can get you?"

"How about the key to this padlock," Fargo said, reaching down to tap it with his finger.

"I don't even know where Father keeps it. Anything besides that?"

Fargo said that he was hungry.

"And it's no wonder. You slept right

through dinner. It's getting late in the afternoon now. There's some cold corn bread left over from breakfast if you'd like that."

Fargo said cold corn bread would be fine with him, and Faith called down to her sisters. Hope came up the ladder, and Prue handed her the corn bread from below.

"You seem to be completely recovered from your cracked noggin, Fargo," Hope said. "I think our little . . . talk was good for you."

"You go on back down," Faith said to her. "I'll do the talking to Fargo now."

Hope laughed and disappeared. Faith gave Fargo the corn bread, and he ate it eagerly. When he'd finished, Faith poured some water in a cup for him.

He drank the water, washing down the corn bread, and handed the cup back to her.

"Samson told me all about your gang and what happened to your mother," he said. "I can't say that I blame him too much for wanting to get back at Ferriday, but I think it's wrong for him to use you to do it."

"We don't have to do it if we don't want to. He's never forced us."

Fargo knew that wasn't exactly true. Samson was their father. He didn't have to get physically abusive. There were other kinds of force.

"Besides," Faith said, "we've never hurt anybody."

"Your sister shot a man yesterday."

"That was different. Prue was saving my life. And even then she didn't kill him. We swore when this started that we'd never kill anybody."

Fargo was glad that the women were as strongly against killing as Samson. Maybe he had a chance of getting out of the cabin alive, after all.

"Sooner or later, something will go wrong," Fargo said.

"No, it won't. You shouldn't say that. It's bad luck. You'll jinx us, like Jonah did to his shipmates."

"Did Samson teach you about the Bible?"

"He's read it a lot. He's named for one of the men in those Bible stories."

"I hope he knows as much about forgiveness as he does about revenge."

"I'm pretty sure he doesn't," Faith said.

Fargo wasn't surprised.

Faith went back down to join her sisters and make supper, and Fargo looked around for a way out of his situation.

He didn't find one. The padlocks were

solid, and the chain was unbreakable. Even if he got the chain off, he'd still have to get past the sisters, but he thought he might be able to do that.

Fargo got up and walked around the bed. He found that he couldn't go far before the chain tightened up on him, and there wasn't anywhere to go, anyway. He was uncomfortable in the loft because, like Samson, he had to stoop. He sat on the edge of the bed facing the dusty little window and looked outside.

He could see the trees along the river and the corral where Samson kept the horses. His Ovaro was there, too.

When he was about to turn back, Fargo noticed something on the rough wooden floor under the window. Lying there was a small piece of metal that might have once been a part of a pin on the back of a broach or something of the sort. Fargo had no idea what kinds of things might have been stored in the loft at one time or another over the years.

He picked up the bit of metal and held it between his thumb and forefinger. It was tarnished but sturdy, and it might do to pick the padlocks. If he could get loose from the chain, all he'd have to do was get his pistol or his knife, or both of them, fight off three women, and get out of there.

That is, if he worked fast he'd have only three women to fight. If he was too slow, there would be four women plus Samson to deal with. The odds weren't good in that case.

They were, however, better odds than he had if he was chained to a rafter. He lifted his ankle and crossed it over the opposite knee, the heavy chain clanking as he did so.

Sitting like that, he inserted the piece of metal into the padlock and twisted it around. The padlock was heavy and crude, and it looked old. Its inner workings might not be in the best of shape, Fargo thought, and that would make his job a little bit easier.

However, it wasn't easy at all. The Trailsman worked at the lock for most of an hour, half listening to the conversation below on the off chance that someone might decide to climb up and visit him.

He'd about given up on the lock when he heard Prue say, "Father and Charity are here."

Fargo had heard nothing that would have indicated their arrival, but he gave up on the lock and put the piece of metal under the bed.

It was a full minute before he heard the

rattle of the wagon that brought Samson and Charity home.

17

Later that evening, Charity brought a plate of beans and meat up to Fargo.

"It's rabbit," she said, as if he couldn't tell. "Hope killed a pair this afternoon."

Fargo had slept so soundly he hadn't heard the shots. Or, he thought, maybe the women had hunted a long way from the house, where he couldn't have heard anything even if he'd been awake. It didn't matter one way or the other, and the rabbit tasted good to him. He was sure that the effects of the gun butt on his head had left him completely.

He ate everything on the plate while Charity watched. When he was finished, she took the plate from him.

"Do you need anything else?" she asked.

"I need to use the outhouse."

"That would be up to Father," Charity said.

She called one of her sisters to take the

plate and climbed back down the ladder. Fargo heard her talking to Samson when she got below, and it wasn't long before Samson loomed over the edge of the loft.

"I still haven't decided what to do with you, Fargo," he said when he stood, slightly bent over, at the foot of the bed. "Kill you or keep you."

"If you're not going to kill me tonight," the Trailsman said, "then you'd better let me use the outhouse. Otherwise, this place won't smell too good by morning."

Samson nodded. He reached into a pocket and brought out a key that he fit into the padlock on the chain hanging over the rafter. There was a click when he turned the key, and the lock opened. Samson removed the lock from the chain and replaced the key in his pocket.

Pulling the chain from the rafter, he said over the sound of its clanking, "I'll pass this end of the chain down to Charity. She'll hold it while you climb down. I'll take it from her and go to the outhouse with you. Prue will have her pistol out. You know what she can do with it."

Fargo touched the side of his head. He also remembered the man Prue had shot. "I know," he said.

"Just wanted to remind you," Samson

said, kneeling down and handing the chain off to Charity, who was standing on the ladder out of sight.

Charity stepped to the floor, and Samson told Fargo to climb down. The Trailsman was a little stiff from being in the bed all day, but aside from that he seemed fine. He didn't feel dizzy at all.

When he was down, he saw the sisters watching him. Prue held the pistol almost casually, but Fargo had an idea she would anticipate any move he made to escape.

Samson joined them on the floor and took the chain.

"Outside, Fargo," he said, and the Trailsman went out the door with Samson coming along behind him, holding the chain up so it wouldn't drag on the ground. Prue stood in the doorway of the cabin with her pistol.

"Just walk slow, Fargo," Samson said.

There wasn't much other way Fargo could walk, not with Samson on the other end of the chain. When they reached the outhouse, Fargo said, "Are you planning to come inside and watch me?"

"That's not funny, Fargo. You just go on in, and if you're shy, you can pull the door shut till it hits the chain."

Fargo wasn't particularly shy, but he

didn't care to have Samson watching him, so he pulled the door almost closed. Then he took care of his business, which was only one of the reasons he was there. The other was that he wanted Samson and the women used to allowing him outside for that purpose. If he ever got the lock picked, he'd make the trip a more interesting one for all concerned.

When he'd finished, Fargo left the outhouse, looking around at the trees, the corral, and the horses. He wanted to be sure where everything was, and by the time he got back to the cabin, he had a pretty clear picture in his mind.

Samson climbed into the loft first, taking the chain from Charity when he was situated. She moved off the ladder, and Fargo went up. When he was situated again, Samson padlocked the chain to the rafter.

"You sleep tight, Fargo," he said, giving the chain a hard jerk to be certain it was secure.

The chain rattled and a little dust drifted down from the roof. A dead bug fell from somewhere and landed on Fargo's bed. Fargo brushed it onto the floor, and Samson went back down the ladder.

Because Fargo seemed fully recovered, no

one sat with him that night. That didn't mean he lacked for visitors. A few hours before dawn he woke to the sound of someone climbing the ladder.

He thought for a second that it might be Samson, coming to do away with him, but as soon as he saw the head poke above the floor of the loft, he knew better.

It was one of the women. She came all the way up and stood beside the bed. It was almost pitch-black, but Fargo thought he knew which one it was.

"Charity?" he said.

"Yes. Are you awake?"

Now that, Fargo thought, was a silly question. But he didn't laugh. He said, "Yes."

"Good. I have something for you."

"What?"

"You'll have to be very quiet."

Fargo moved on the bed, and the corn shucks rustled like dead leaves in the wind.

"I'll be quiet," he said. "The bed might not."

"Father's a sound sleeper. Take off your clothes."

"Can't. I have a chain on my ankle. You want to unlock it?"

"You managed just fine with Hope."

Fargo sat up on the bed. "Don't you four have anything better to talk about than me?"

"We don't all talk about you. Prue's not interested." Charity reached down and took hold of the linen shift she was wearing. She slipped it over her head. "Are you interested, Fargo?"

Even in the dim light Fargo could see the round curves of her hips, the soft globes of her breasts. He was interested, all right.

"Well?" she said.

Fargo sat up and took off his shirt. He moved to the side of the bed, stood up, and pushed his pants down.

Charity groped for him in the darkness, found him, and gave him a squeeze.

"You're interested. Come here."

She pulled him closer and took a firmer grip on his erect pole. She slipped the tip into the nest of wiry hair between her legs and moved it around. She was already slick, and she moaned her pleasure.

Fargo hoped she was right about her father being a sound sleeper, but just in case she was wrong, he pulled her to him and kissed her.

Keeping Fargo trapped between her legs, she responded eagerly, her hips writhing as they kissed. Little moans escaped even though their mouths were locked together.

Charity pressed herself against Fargo so hard that he was forced backward. When his calves touched the side of the bed, he sat down abruptly, releasing Charity, who stood above him.

She didn't stand for long. Seeing that he was sitting on the edge of the bed, she straddled him and lowered herself onto him.

He penetrated her easily, and she slid down his pole, settling on his lap. For a short while she simply sat there, pressing her breasts into his chest.

"Umm," she said, very softly.

After a few seconds, she moved back a bit, swaying her upper body from side to side, letting her jutting nipples graze Fargo lightly.

That procedure didn't last long. She began to move on his lap, and before long it was almost as if she were churning butter. She threw her head back, whipping her hair, her mouth open in a soundless scream of pleasure. Fargo had to put his hands on her hips to keep her from lifting herself completely off him as his own pleasure built to the bursting point.

The corn shucks rustled beneath them.

When the time came that he could hold back no longer, Fargo pulled her firmly to him, and as she squirmed against him he came in ropy streams. She lowered her head and bit his shoulder to keep from crying out, her fingers gripping his naked back.

They were both wrung out when it was over, but for a while Charity didn't move. She sat there with Fargo still inside her until he started to grow firm again. She moved her hips, and Fargo couldn't help but respond. He bounced a little off the side of the bed, and soon they were in rhythm, pumping and thrusting, the shucks crunching under Fargo's naked bottom. In a short while, they both exploded for a second time, and again Charity had to sink her teeth into Fargo's shoulder to keep herself silent.

They sat quietly for several minutes. Charity finally stood up and put her gown back on.

"I would purely hate it if anything happened to you, Fargo," she said. "We all would."

Fargo wasn't so sure that the *we* included Prue and Samson, but he didn't argue the point. He put his clothing back on and was asleep not more than a minute after Charity descended the ladder.

The next day Hope went into town with Samson, and no one came to the loft to visit Fargo other than to give him breakfast. He figured they'd found out what they wanted to know about him and were satisfied. He was, too, for the time being, though he did remain a bit curious about Prue. Maybe he'd find out about her in time, but if the truth were known, he'd rather get away from the cabin before that happened.

He located the piece of metal under the bed and got to work on the lock. He told himself that he'd get it open eventually. After that, he'd have to trust luck and opportunity.

18

The guard on the day's run was a man named Moss. Dobkins recognized him as soon as he walked into the saloon and bought a drink at the bar.

"What the hell is he doing here?" he said aloud.

"Who?" Fowler said.

Dobkins pointed out Moss and said, "Name's Moss. He's the stage guard on today's run. He's not supposed to be here."

The stage station wasn't far, only about a quarter of a mile, but the drivers and guards usually stayed there and didn't go wandering off.

Fowler nodded in the direction of the table where Hope was holding court with eight or ten men. "Maybe he heard about her," he said.

Dobkins had been wondering about the woman. Yesterday a different woman had been in the saloon, but the two looked somewhat alike even though their hair color was different. The one yesterday had been dark, and this one was blonde, but Dobkins thought they were probably sisters.

While he was thinking about that, Moss got a whiskey and walked over to the table where the blonde was telling some story that was making the men laugh. Dobkins knew they would have laughed even if she'd been telling them what she'd had for breakfast. Moss tried to ease close to the table, but a couple of the men pushed him back.

The blonde stopped talking and looked around. Seeing Moss, she said something to the men and one of them let Moss have his seat. Dobkins figured that Moss knew the woman and that she'd told the other man that Moss wouldn't be there long. Which made Dobkins wonder if Moss often visited the saloon when the stage stopped in Laramie. It wasn't unlikely, as there was plenty of time during the stop. Probably nobody would even notice that he'd gone if he got back on time. And that set Dobkins' mind wandering down another track entirely.

Dobkins didn't think Moss would recognize him as long as he didn't get too close. They'd met only once, and Dobkins had been wearing his dude clothes. Still,

Dobkins didn't want to take any chances. He told Fowler that he was leaving.

Fowler shrugged. "You can go if you want to. I'm stickin' right here. I'll watch and see what goes on with Moss and the woman."

"I'll be back. Don't do anything without me."

"You're the boss."

Dobkins nodded and left. He wanted to go back to the room at the hotel and mull things over for a while. Moss and the woman had given him a lot to think about.

Dobkins had guessed right about Moss. On a run a few weeks earlier he'd heard about the beautiful young women who frequented the Red Dog Saloon. The rumor going around the fort was that occasionally a man could get some special attention from one or another of them if he had a good story to tell, and Moss thought he'd have a look at the women and see what there was to see.

The first one he'd seen had been Hope, and he'd been surprised at how pretty she was. He didn't get much notice from her, but her sister Faith, whom he'd met later on, had flattered him and hinted that if he ever had any really interesting news from Saint Jo, she might let him get her alone somewhere. Just what would happen then hadn't been specified, but Moss' imagination had flamed at the thought.

That was all the encouragement Moss had needed. He was a stringy, sour-looking man with droopy eyelids and a hooked nose. Women didn't much take to him, so a kind word and a smile were all that he required to get his hopes up. Every time he had a stopover at Laramie he was in the saloon with whatever interesting news he could glean back in Missouri. So far it hadn't done him any good.

But today, for the first time, he had something that would do the trick, or so he thought. It was the very thing to get him alone with the blond beauty, and who knew what might happen after that?

Moss was naturally pleased when Hope made one of her admirers give up his seat for him. He thought he already had a head start, what with her being so partial to him, and he imagined what Hope would look like with her clothes lying scattered around on the floor of a room somewhere. Just the thought of that scene was enough to get him all stirred up inside.

When Moss sat down and Hope looked at him, it was like they were the only two people at the crowded table. That got him even more excited, and he could hardly stop himself from blurting out his news.

He managed to hold it in, however, and when she asked him what was happening back east, he just said, "Lots of things. Mighty interestin' things."

She drew her chair a little closer to his and looked at him with lowered eyes.

"What kind of things? And how interesting?"

"The kind of things I can't talk about here," Moss said, looking around before taking a big swallow of his drink. "Too important."

A few of the men started to razz Moss about that, joshing him that he didn't know anything that the rest of them didn't know.

"You're just tryin' to get Hope to let you talk a walk with her," one man said. "Tryin' to get her away from the rest of us fellas."

The others joined in the fun, and Moss tried to shut them up by saying his intentions were only of the best. It didn't work. The men just got more boisterous.

Moss looked at Hope and raised his voice a bit.

"They don't know what they're talkin' about," he said. "But I do."

He did, too. He hoped she could see that. And apparently she could. She stood up and said, "It's such a nice day. Would you like to go for a walk, Mr. Moss?"

Moss stood up and found that his knees were a little watery. He didn't mind. This was about the best thing that had happened to him in a long time. He poured the rest of the drink down his throat and swallowed.

"I'd be mighty pleased to walk with you," he said.

Hope wasn't often fooled by men. She'd never thought much about Moss before, and never really thought he'd have anything to say that was worth hearing. But she'd been wrong. She was sure he had something to tell her that she should know about. It was a hunch, maybe, but it was more than that. There was something about the earnestness in his voice, an earnestness tinged with a little bit of something like fear. She didn't know what it was he had to tell her, but she knew she wanted to hear it, whatever it was.

She didn't intend to do much to get it, however. She had a feeling that Moss wanted nothing more in the world than to get her alone in a room and get her naked.

She wasn't opposed to that if she had to do it to get the information she wanted. It could even be fun, as it had been with Fargo. But not with someone like Moss, not if she could avoid it.

She thought about Fargo: how big he was, how strong and straight. She wouldn't mind getting him alone again, but Moss was scrawny and none too clean. He was also a good fifteen years older than she was. Talking was as far as it was going, she told herself, confident that she could get whatever she wanted from him with little more than a smile.

She was right about it, too. Moss was like a puppy, following her along as they left the saloon, so eager to please her that he was almost babbling.

"I do know some good stuff," he said as soon as they were out the door. "It's mighty interestin', too. Not the usual kind of news you hear. You might say it's a secret."

That caught Hope's attention. She put a hand on his arm and gave him her best smile.

At that little bit of attention, his own smile stretched his face so much that Hope thought it might split. She was afraid he might pass out from sheer happiness. For just a second she felt sorry for the way she was using him, but the feeling passed as quickly as it had come.

"You're going to tell me what this big news is, aren't you?" she said. "Even if it's a secret?"

"Yes, ma'am, I surely am. But maybe not here. Maybe we could go . . . somewhere there ain't so many folks around."

Hope waved a hand. "There's no one here except us."

The wagons of the pilgrims were a hundred yards away, as were the fort's buildings, and the Palace was a good thirty. The stores were closer, but no one was standing outside them.

"You can tell me right here," Hope said. "I know it's a good story."

"I thought maybe, well . . ." Moss' voice trailed off, and he lowered his head.

Hope patted his arm. "You're a wonderful storyteller, I'm certain. You can probably sweep a girl off her feet with just a few words."

Moss's head lifted, and there was a spark in his eyes.

"Why don't you see what you can do?" Hope said. "I'd like to hear you talk."

"Well, it's something I'm not supposed to tell anybody. How's that for a start?"

"A very good one." Hope was getting impatient. "Go on. I can hardly wait to hear."

"All right," Moss said. "I'll tell you."

And he did.

■ ■ ■ ■

Moss had been lounging on the boardwalk out in front of the stage office in Saint Jo when he'd heard three men talking inside. He hadn't been supposed to overhear, but once he'd heard what they had to say, he couldn't very well forget it. He didn't even try, since he knew it would make such a good tale to tell Hope when he got to Laramie.

One of the men doing the talking had been Mr. Ferriday. Moss didn't recognize any of the other voices.

"Nobody's to know what's on the coach," Mr. Ferriday had said. "Not even the driver or the guards. This is strictly between us."

"Are you sure about that?" someone had said. "It might be a good idea to tell them."

"I don't want them getting any ideas." It had been Ferriday again. "We don't usually haul cargo this valuable."

"But what if there's trouble?"

"There won't be any trouble."

"I've heard some things about this run that have made me uneasy. You've had some robberies."

"You don't have to worry. That was all small stuff, involving the passengers. I've sent a man out there to take care of that situation."

"But has he done it?"

"He's a good man."

"That doesn't answer the question."

"I've told you not to worry about it." Ferriday's voice had gotten sharp. "That should be enough for you."

"It's a heavy cargo. Won't somebody get suspicious?"

"I don't think so," Ferriday had said. "You let me worry about that."

Moss could think of only one thing that would be that heavy, or at least only one thing that would cause a discussion like the one he'd just heard.

Moss knew it was against the company's policy to carry anything valuable, but this time was an exception for some reason. Taking care not to be heard, Moss quietly slipped away, thinking of how Hope's face would look when he told her, and of how impressed she would be.

Hope was impressed, all right, and not just for the reasons Moss might have expected.

"Was that a good story?" he said when he was finished with the telling.

"It most certainly was," Hope said. She leaned toward him and gave him a kiss on his grubby cheek.

Moss beamed and Hope thought he might dance a little jig, like a performer in a medicine show.

While he was still basking in the glow of her admiration, she led him back toward the saloon.

"Isn't it time you headed for the station?" she said. "You know the stage can't leave without you. You're an important man."

Moss's puny chest swelled as much as it was capable of.

"You got that right. They can't make the run without me. But I'll be back in a few days. I'll see you again when I come through, I reckon."

"Either me or one of my sisters. I'll tell them all about you."

Moss was practically strutting now.

"You be sure and do that," he said.

19

Unlike Faith, Hope didn't make Samson wait to hear what she'd learned.

"Gold, you think?" he said after she'd told him.

The wagon bounced as a wheel dropped into a hole, and Hope grabbed the seat to steady herself.

"What else could it be?" she said.

"If it is, it's what I've been waiting for — a chance to get back at Ferriday so he'll really suffer. I'm suspicious, though. He won't usually carry gold. It's against the rules of his stage line."

"That's what Moss said. This is some kind of special occasion."

"And it's coming through tomorrow?"

"According to Moss. It's going to be mighty dangerous to try for it."

"How do you figure that?" Samson said.

"You have to think it'll be heavily guarded. They won't be taking any chances, and they know we've been stopping stages around here."

"We'll just have to take the chance," Samson said.

Hope knew he didn't really mean the *we*. He never went on their raids. She and her sisters would be the ones taking the chance.

"There's a little more to the story," she said, and in fact she'd held back the part of what Moss had said that interested her most.

"More? What more could there be?"

"Moss said something about Ferriday sending a man out here to look into the robberies and put a stop to them."

"He was lying. Nobody's come along and looked into anything, much less put a stop to them."

"That's where you're wrong," Hope said. "Somebody's come along, all right, and we have him at the cabin."

"Damn, girl," Samson said. "You think Fargo was sent here to catch us?"

"Yes, I do. That would explain a lot of things. Fargo never did tell us what he was doing when we caught him sneaking around the house. He wasn't there by accident, that's for sure, and we know he followed us from where we robbed the stage. Why didn't he interfere when he had the chance, unless he wanted to find out more about us? I'm sure he's the one working for Ferriday."

Samson was silent for a while as the wagon bounced along. Finally he said, "I think you're right. Now the question is, what do we do about Mr. Fargo? He's turned out to be even more trouble than I thought he'd be."

Hope didn't know what Samson would decide, but she didn't like the look on his face or the way he remained silent for the rest of the ride home.

Dobkins was back at the saloon when Moss and the blonde returned from their walk. Moss came inside for one last drink before returning to the stage station. He told the blonde good-bye and went to the bar. She went back to her table and was immediately swarmed by eight or ten men.

"What do we do now?" Fowler said when Dobkins sat down.

The plan had been for Fowler to lure the guard away from the stage and disable him when the gold shipment came along. If killing him was necessary, then Fowler would kill him and take his place as guard.

To ensure that he got the job, Fowler had been provided with a badly forged letter, supposedly from Ferriday. After the guard was incapacitated, Fowler would show up at the station, hear to his surprise that the guard was missing, and present the letter, claiming that he was on the way to Oregon to take a job as a guard there.

Dobkins believed the letter would be enough to assure Fowler of being installed as the guard. Later, the letter would be easily proved to be a fake so that Ferriday wouldn't be implicated. By that time, however, Fowler would be long gone, and the gold as well.

"I've changed the plan," Dobkins said. "We're not going to do anything about the guard tomorrow. You and I are going to be on the stage as passengers."

"The hell you say."

"Look," Dobkins said. "Fargo's gone. I don't know what happened to the bastard, but we're not going to be able to pin the robbery on him."

Fowler had been thinking it over and wanted to know why not. "After all," Fowler said, "he's not around, and folks already think he's behind things. He's perfect for taking the blame."

"Not if we don't have a body to leave behind," Dobkins reminded him. "And if he turns up with an alibi later on, what then?"

"Damn," Fowler said, getting the point.

"All right, then, what are we gonna do?"

"I think we'll be able to pin the blame for the robbery on someone else."

"Who would that be?"

"That woman over there."

"You're jokin' with me, Dobkins. I don't like jokes."

"I'm not joking." Dobkins kept his voice level. "She's mixed up with the robbers somehow. I'm sure of it."

Fowler looked disbelieving. "Why's that?"

"Think about it, Fowler. She's here all the time. And just look at those fools around her. They'd tell her anything to get her attention. What better way to get information about the stage and what the passengers are carrying?"

Fowler twisted his beer mug in his hands and nodded slowly. "I see what you're getting at. But how does it change things?"

"The outlaw gang will hit the stage tomorrow. Moss must have found out about the gold. Why else would a woman like her take him for a walk? We'll have to be ready for them, and we'll warn the driver and the guard."

"Maybe they won't believe us."

"You have that letter. They'll trust us enough to be wary of the gang." Dobkins paused to gather his thoughts. "Now. You know the gang doesn't kill people. Doesn't even hurt them. That means we'll have the advantage of them. We'll start shooting as soon as they get close enough. We'll kill all of them."

Fowler was catching on. "And then we'll take care of the guard and the driver."

Dobkins smiled. "Right. We'll hide the gold and a couple of the bodies, and claim that two of the robbers got away with the loot."

"I guess that could work. Mighty dangerous, though. A man should get a little extra for something like that."

Dobkins' smile grew wider. "I think that can be arranged."

Dobkins didn't mind promising Fowler whatever he wanted. His plan was that Fowler wouldn't be around to collect.

"Just one little problem that I see," Fowler said.

"What's that?"

"What if the gang don't show up? Who you gonna blame then?"

Dobkins hadn't even considered that possibility because he was completely convinced that the gang would rob the stage. He forced himself to think about what would happen if he was wrong. After a minute or so it came to him.

"I don't think we have to worry," he said. "But if they don't show up, we'll blame them for it. The gold will be gone, and the driver and the guard will be dead. It would be better if we had a body or two for proof that we fought off the robbers, but if we don't, then we'll just send a posse after them."

Fowler said, "They'll claim they didn't do it."

"Who'll believe them? If the shooting starts as soon as they're spotted, they'll fight back. Maybe some of them will die. Maybe all of them. Doesn't matter. If they fight, and they will, everybody will be convinced they're guilty."

"How can you be sure they'll fight?"

"Because we'll be in the posse, and we'll shoot first."

"I guess that might work."

"Damn right it will," Dobkins said. "It has to."

"You know how it is with a bad dog?" Samson said.

They were getting near the cabin, and Hope didn't like his tone.

"I don't understand," she said. "What dog are you talking about?"

"Just any dog. Sometimes one turns on

184

you, and you have to put him down. It's not like you were takin' any pleasure in the killing. It's just a job that you have to do."

"If you're talking about Fargo, you're wrong. He didn't turn on us. He was just doing a job. It would be just as wrong to kill him as it would to kill anybody else."

Samson didn't say anything, and Hope could see that he wasn't convinced. She'd have to get her sisters on her side, she thought. Surely all of them together could save Fargo.

"I don't hold with killin'," Samson said. "You know that. But this is different."

"I don't believe that."

Samson looked straight ahead and didn't answer. He didn't say another word until they got back to the cabin.

Fargo spent most of the day working on the lock. Several times he'd thought he almost had it open, but each time he'd been wrong. He'd gotten tantalizingly close, but now his fingers were cramping from his efforts, and he was still no closer to being free than he'd been that morning.

The sisters had spent a lot of the afternoon fishing in the river, and Fargo had hoped to be able to get away before they returned to the house. It hadn't worked out. They'd returned and were talking together.

He heard Prue's voice announce that the wagon would soon be there, and he put the pin back beneath the bed and lay down, wondering what would happen next.

It was getting on toward sundown, but the sky was darker than it should have been. Fargo sat up and looked out the window. Clouds were massing on the horizon, and the Trailsman knew that a storm would be rolling in sometime during the evening.

That was all to the good, he thought, if he could get free. If the storm was noisy enough, he might be able to escape the cabin and get to the horses before anybody even knew he was gone.

But first he'd have to get that pesky lock opened.

The wagon rolled into the yard, and Hope came inside the cabin while Samson attended to the horse. The women all started to talk at once, and Fargo heard his name mentioned a time or two. Then Charity came up into the loft to talk to him. She didn't waste any time getting to the point.

"Father's planning to kill you," she said.

"And here I thought maybe you came up to tell me what's for supper."

"Fried fish, that's what. We caught a nice

mess of catfish today." Charity shook her head. "How can you wonder about supper with what I just told you?"

"A man's going to die, he ought to think about his last meal."

Charity smiled. "Is that all he should think about?"

"I don't know. You got something better in mind?"

"You're hard to figure, Fargo. If someone had given me the news you just got, I'd be at least a little bit scared."

"I'm scared," Fargo said. "But I'm hungry, too."

He was half listening to the conversation below and heard the word *gold,* followed by the word *stagecoach.*

"Sounds to me like there's more going on than just my execution," he said.

"There is. But you don't need to know about it, even if you were sent here by Ferriday to stop us."

Fargo didn't bother to deny it. He asked how she knew.

"Hope figured it out. I want you to know that we're going to try to save you, but we might not be able to. Father's hard to change when he's made up his mind."

"Well, I appreciate the thought, anyway," Fargo told her. "I really do. Maybe you can throw an extra piece of fish on my plate?"

"You beat everything, Fargo," Charity said, and went back down the ladder.

When she was gone, Fargo moved over to the edge of the loft and listened to the conversation below. Samson came in, and for a minute everyone talked at once. Then Samson said, "Listen to me."

He didn't raise his voice, but they all heard him and the chatter died.

"You're going to take that coach tomorrow, just like all the others," Samson said. "It won't be any different, except for the gold. Don't even worry with the passengers. Just get that gold and come straight back here."

"What about Fargo?" Hope said.

"Never you mind. I'll see to him."

The women argued for several minutes, but Samson didn't respond. They finally gave up, and Fargo figured his fate was decided.

Prue said, "I don't like it."

Her voice was clear and strong, and Fargo heard a strange note in it.

"It's not yours to decide," Samson said. "I'll take care of Fargo, and that's all there is to it."

"I'm not talking about Fargo."

"What do you mean?"

"I'm talking about the robbery. I don't like it."

"Why not?" Samson was indignant. "It's what I've been waiting for — a chance to hurt Ferriday bad. And we'll be rich when all's said and done."

"I don't think so."

"What do you think, then?"

"I think most of us will be dead," Prue said.

20

The storm broke around midnight. Fargo had been working with the pin since supper, which had been fried catfish rolled in cornmeal. The cabin still smelled like fish, but Fargo didn't mind. The food had been delicious, the white meat of the fish hot and tender. If it were his last meal, it had been a mighty fine one.

Fargo didn't intend for it to be his last meal, though, not if he could help it. He kept working with the pin, and after another half hour, he finally opened the lock. It happened all at once, as easily as if he'd used the key. He didn't know what he'd done that was different from all the other tries he'd made, and he didn't care. He opened the lock and removed the chain from around his leg.

Lightning flashed outside, illuminating the cabin brightly for a second. Fargo saw nobody down below. Samson was in his room and the women in theirs, presumably sleeping soundly as the thunder rumbled overhead.

Fargo knew where his knife and pistol were, he thought, in a cabinet against one wall. It was the only place in the cabin to put anything.

Holding his boots clasped under his arm, Fargo went down the ladder and padded over to the cabinet. Sure enough, his pistol and knife were inside. So was his hat. He put down the boots and strapped the gun belt around his waist. Then he put on the boots and slipped the knife into the right one. He looked around for his big Henry rifle, but it was nowhere to be seen. Samson might have taken it into his room, Fargo thought. He hated to leave it, but he didn't have time to look for it, and he didn't want to disturb the sleepers by moving around too much. He'd just have to leave it behind. He pulled his hat down low over his face.

Rain lashed the cabin as Fargo made his way across the room. He waited for thunder and opened the door, stepping out into the storm. He headed straight for the corral, not knowing where his saddle might be. He'd ride bareback if he had to. Wind whipped the rain into him, hard as little stones, and the ground was getting slick with mud. Fargo pulled his hat lower and tighter.

He never heard the cabin door open, nor did he hear Samson coming up behind him. The only excuse he could offer was that the noise of the storm drowned out the sounds.

While his hearing might not have been up to par, however, there was nothing wrong with his feeling. He knew at once when Samson's huge hand clasped his shoulder.

"Where the hell do you think you're goin', Fargo?" Samson said.

Fargo had no trouble hearing that voice above the sound of the wind and the rain. He didn't bother to answer the question. He whirled and hammered Samson in the chest as hard as he could, right about on his heart.

The big man was staggered, and Fargo took advantage by hitting him again, this time in the stomach.

Samson folded in the middle, and Fargo was about to flatten him with a blow to the back of the head when he heard Prue say, "Don't do that."

She was standing not far away, the rain pelting her and blowing her hair. The weather had no effect on her grip on the pistol she held. It was pointed right at Fargo's head, which twinged a little at the thought of what Prue had already done to it.

Fargo stayed his hand. Samson remained bent, struggling to catch his breath.

"Back up," Prue said, and Fargo knew she wasn't talking to Samson. Looking over her shoulder, he could see her sisters crowded into the doorway, watching them.

Fargo looked at Samson. "I thought you were supposed to be a sound sleeper."

Samson straightened a bit, but he was still having trouble catching his breath. Rain streamed down his face and plastered his long hair to him.

"You . . . should have stayed . . . inside."

"Yeah," Fargo said. "I might have done that, except that you were planning to kill me."

"Come back to the cabin," Prue said.

That sounded like a good idea to Fargo. He wiped rain off his face and walked past Samson. When he got to Prue, she said, "I'll take your pistol."

He drew it and handed it to her, butt first.

She took it with her free hand, stuck it in her waistband, and said, "Now the knife."

"I don't think you have room for it."

"Charity does. Come here, Charity."

The brunette left the shelter of the doorway and took Fargo's knife after he removed it from his boot.

"I'm wet," Fargo said. "I'm going inside."

"Go ahead," Prue said, turning to walk behind him, the gun focused on the base of his spine.

Inside the cabin Fargo ignored the sisters and climbed up to the loft. He removed his buckskins and dried himself off as best he could with the quilt from the bed. Then he lay down on the mattress to wait for whatever came next.

Samson came back to the cabin and lit a lamp. When he got it burning, he told the women to get back to bed. They returned to their room and Samson climbed up the ladder to the loft.

"Cover yourself, Fargo," he said. Water still ran out of his long hair and dripped on the floor.

Fargo lay where he was and looked up at the shadows thrown by the lamp as they danced on the underside of the roof.

Samson picked up the ragged quilt with one hand and threw it over Fargo. He held a pistol in his other hand.

"I ought to kill you right now," he said.

"But you won't," Fargo said.

"No, I won't. My girls are against it, and I don't want to kill you here in front of them."

"They're not here."

194

"They're right down below. It's the same thing."

"You'll wait until they're gone tomorrow and do it then, I guess."

"You guess right, but there's no use in you tellin' that to anybody."

"You know something, Samson, you should think hard about what Prue said, about everybody getting killed."

"You don't believe that stuff do you, Fargo? She's made some guesses that turned out right, sure, but that don't mean there'll be any trouble tomorrow."

Thunder rumbled across the sky, but it was more distant now as the storm moved on. Fargo sat up on the side of the bed and pulled the quilt around him.

"I've seen and heard enough from Prue to believe she can sense things that maybe the rest of us can't," he said. "I think you should listen to her."

"The stage has one guard and a driver," Samson said. "How much trouble can they give?"

"Plenty. And how do you know there'll be just one guard?"

"Always is."

"That doesn't mean it'll be the same, not with a gold shipment. They'll have extra men on the stage, and all of them will be armed. They'll kill those women before they even get close to the gold."

"That shipment's a secret. Nobody's to know about it, and they won't want to tip it off by putting on extra guards."

"Now *you're* guessing," Fargo said. "And who's to say you're better at it than Prue?"

"You hush that kind of talk. It's bad luck, and I don't want to hear it. I'm gonna chain you up now. I don't know how you got loose, but you'd best not try it again. I'll kill you if you do."

He called for Charity, and she climbed up to hold the pistol on Fargo while Samson put the chain around his ankle and fastened it with the padlock.

Fargo knew that even if he subdued the big man and got past Charity, Prue would be waiting for him when he descended the ladder.

"You might as well get some sleep," Samson said when he finished. "No need spendin' your last night on earth worryin' about what's to come."

"You're a real comfort," Fargo said.

"I try to be," Samson said, and he went down the ladder.

Charity gave Fargo a pitying look and followed her father.

■ ■ ■ ■

The next day was bright and sunny. The storm had left the air fresh and brought a sharp coolness down from the mountains. Dobkins thought it was just about a perfect day for a stagecoach robbery.

It was too bad that Hal Calhoun wasn't cooperating.

"I got a letter right here in my hand from the stage company," Calhoun said, waving the paper in Dobkins' face. "Driver brought it in with him. Says plain as day, 'No passengers.' "

"We're not passengers," Dobkins said. "We're representatives of Mr. Ferriday. Mr. Fowler has a letter of his own."

Fowler dug the letter out of his shirt and handed it to Calhoun, who read it slowly and carefully, moving his lips for every word, and then handed it back.

"Maybe you're gonna be a guard when you get to Oregon," Calhoun said, giving Fowler a hard look, "and maybe you ain't. Don't matter to me even a little bit. You ain't gettin' there on this stage."

Dobkins had at one time admired employees who were loyal to the company's policies, but he thought Calhoun was taking things a little too far.

"Do you know who I am?" he said.

"Yeah, as a matter of fact, I do. You're Mr. Larry Forbess."

Dobkins was taken aback until he remembered that he'd given Calhoun a false name at their first meeting. He said, "No. I am Samuel Dobkins."

"Bullshit," Calhoun said. He'd obviously heard the name before.

"It's true," Dobkins said. "I gave you a false name because I'm here on a special assignment for Mr. Ferriday himself. You don't know it, but there's a certain cargo on the stage that has to be protected from bandits at all costs. Mr. Fowler and I are going along from this point on to see to it that nothing happens to that cargo."

"It's easy enough to claim to be somebody you ain't," Calhoun said. "How do I know you're who you say you are?"

"Why don't we talk to the driver and the guard?" Dobkins asked. "That should settle it."

"All right, then. We'll do that."

They walked over to the stagecoach, which was painted red with yellow trim. The white oak wheels were muddy, and they'd flung mud on the sides of the stage as well.

The driver was inside the station, but the

guard, a man named Avinger, hadn't left his place on the stage. He was still up in the box, in the shotgun seat, with his shotgun resting across his knees.

"We need to talk to you," Dobkins said.

Avinger gave them a suspicious look. "What about?"

"It's about the shipment."

The guard cocked the shotgun. "What do you know about that?"

Dobkins looked at Calhoun. "See? I told you it was a special shipment."

Calhoun seemed surprised at the guard's reaction. "Yeah, maybe you were right."

"There's no maybe to it." Dobkins turned back to the guard. "I'm Samuel Dobkins. Mr. Ferriday sent me and this man here" — he pointed to Fowler — "to provide some extra firepower in case there is a robbery. This is a dangerous area you're passing through."

The guard spit a brown stream of tobacco juice over the side of the coach. "I've heard about the robberies," he said, "and I've heard of you. Maybe we met once in Saint Jo."

If they'd met, Dobkins didn't remember it, but that didn't matter. He said, "I'm sure we did. Calhoun here doesn't want us to ride along with you. He thinks we're not who we say we are."

"Well, he can rest easy on that," the guard responded. "You're Dobkins, all right."

"I guess you can go along, then," Calhoun said, giving in. "Since he's willin' to vouch for you, it oughta be all right. If you're gonna be any help, though, you need to be armed. You got any guns?"

"We do," Dobkins said. "Fowler, go get them."

Fowler left, and Calhoun said, "Prob'ly won't be any trouble anyway. No way anybody could've found out about this shipment, whatever it is."

"You're right," Dobkins said, "but there's no use in taking chances, and Mr. Ferriday sent us to ride along. So that's what we're going to do."

Fowler returned with their guns, a Henry rifle and a shotgun.

"That oughta be enough firepower to take care of any bandits you run into, all right," Calhoun said.

"Oh, I think you can count on that," Dobkins told him.

21

The women seemed nervous to Fargo, but he didn't know that they weren't nervous every time they went out. They talked a lot, and their voices were loud. But not Prue's. Fargo listened as he lay on his bed, but he couldn't hear her voice at all. As far as Fargo could tell, she didn't have anything to say.

He heard Samson give them some last-minute instructions, telling them to come straight back to the cabin, and they said that of course they would.

Hope was going to drive the wagon to bring the gold back in. They wouldn't be able to carry it on horseback. Her horse would be tied behind the wagon so she could ride out to face the coach with the others.

While they were outside getting ready, Prue came back into the cabin.

"Fargo?" she said. "You up there?"

That was as bad as Charity asking if he was awake, he thought. Where else could he be?

"I'm here," he said.

"I'm coming up."

When she was in the loft, she looked Fargo over. He was partially covered by the quilt. Fargo wondered what she had in mind.

"You should get dressed," she said, contrary to Fargo's expectations. She wasn't like her sisters at all. "Your clothing's dry by now."

"Is that what you came up here to tell me?" If Fargo was disappointed, he didn't show it. He moved his leg and rattled the chain. "I can't get my pants on over this thing."

"Oh. I'm sorry. I wanted to tell you that something's wrong with this robbery."

"Hell," Fargo said. "I know that. You four aren't cut out for the job."

"That's not what I'm talking about. It's something else. It's going wrong, and I think you're part of the reason that it is."

Fargo sat up on the bed, keeping the quilt draped over his lower body, and reached down to rattle the chain again.

"I'm not part of anything," he said. "Except being a prisoner."

"You don't understand what I'm trying to tell you. You might be a prisoner, but you're involved in this robbery somehow. It's a feeling I have."

"I have a feeling you're wrong."

"I wish I were. It's not going to turn out well. That's the part that's your fault."

Fargo just looked at her.

"It is," she insisted. "I don't know how or why, but it is."

"It's not," Fargo said, "but even if it was, there's nothing I can do about it, unless you want to take this chain off my leg."

"You can talk to Father. Maybe you can convince him that the robbery is a mistake."

"That's more in your line," Fargo said. "Anyway, I've already tried that. Samson didn't want to hear anything I had to say about it."

"He's stubborn," Prue admitted. "I'm afraid he's going to be sorry later that he didn't listen."

There wasn't much Fargo could do about that. He shrugged.

"I'm sorry," he said.

"No you're not," Prue said. "You don't give a damn. What happens to us doesn't matter to you."

"I'm the one Samson's planning to kill," Fargo reminded her. "I don't see you doing a whole lot about that."

Prue was going to say more, maybe in an attempt to defend herself and her sisters, but her father called her from the doorway.

"Get on down here, Prue. It's time for you girls to move out."

Prue took a last look at Fargo and shook her head. Then she turned and went down the ladder without another word.

Fargo waited until she was outside. Then he reached down and undid the padlock. He'd spent most of the night working on it, and it had been a little easier to open this time. He removed the chain and got dressed. He was just finishing up when he heard the women ride away.

He lay back down on the bed and covered himself with the quilt, careful to place the end of the chain under the quilt so that it would appear to be still attached to his leg. That done, he waited.

In a few minutes Samson came back into the cabin. Fargo heard him moving around down below. Fargo knew it wouldn't be long before Samson climbed up to the loft, and he wouldn't be coming to swap tales or to give Fargo a cup of coffee.

Sure enough, in a little while Samson's big head appeared. The rest of him soon followed. He had a pistol in a holster that was belted around his immense girth.

"Mornin', Fargo," he said.

Fargo didn't bother to respond.

"No need to swell up like a dead frog," Samson said. "It's not like I'm gonna enjoy what I have to do."

"You'll get my blood on the bed if you do it here," Fargo said.

"Don't plan to do it here. Thought I'd take you outside. It's a nice day, and I don't want to have to clean up any mess you make."

"I don't think I'll go outside."

Samson drew the pistol. "I think you will."

"You can threaten me, but you can't make me go. You'll just have to shoot me here."

"Dammit, Fargo, you get out of that bed."

"You have me chained up," Fargo said. "I couldn't go anywhere even if I wanted to. And I don't want to."

Samson thought that over. He holstered the pistol and said, "I'll let you loose, but I'll be holding the end of the chain. So don't try to get away."

"I'm not going to try to get away. I'm not even going to move."

"That's what you think," Samson said. "If you don't want to come, then by God I'll just drag you. It's a long fall from this loft.

You might just be dead before I get you out the door."

With that, Samson reached into a pocket for the key. To get to the padlock on the chain hanging over the rafter, he had to raise his arms and turn a little away from Fargo.

That was what Fargo had been waiting for. He jumped from the bed, throwing the quilt over Samson and turning the big man around to disorient him.

Samson jerked about and fired the pistol through the quilt. Pieces of cloth flew like snow, and the quilt caught fire from the muzzle flash. The bullet missed Fargo, who was already halfway down the ladder.

Samson thrashed around the loft, trying to get the burning quilt off, fighting it as if it were an animal that had attacked him. The pistol discharged again.

Fargo was on the floor when that happened. He crossed the cabin's big room and retrieved his pistol and knife. When he had them, he started for the door.

He almost got there before Samson crashed down upon him, still wrapped in the quilt, which was trailing smoke. Along with him came the chair that had been in the loft.

Fargo figured that Samson had stumbled

blindly over the side of the loft. He'd grabbed at the chair and brought it down with him. It hit the floor at almost the same time he did.

He didn't land squarely on top of Fargo, but caught the backs of his legs and brought him to the floor anyway.

The Trailsman sprawled out on his face. Samson rolled off him, throwing the quilt into the air as he did so.

The quilt flapped down like a colorful bird and settled over Fargo as Samson looked around for the pistol that had fallen from his hand when he fell.

Fargo threw off the quilt. His own pistol had scooted out of its holster and across the room. Fargo spotted it under a chair and started to worm forward.

Samson's boot smashed down on Fargo's hand.

"Stop right there," Samson said.

Fargo glanced up. The big man didn't have his pistol, but he was grinding the Trailsman's hand into the floor with the sole of his boot.

Fargo grabbed Samson's leg with his free hand and jerked. He might as well have been jerking on a deep-rooted tree. Samson didn't budge. Keeping his foot on Fargo's hand, he reached down for the Trailsman, aiming to get his own hands around Fargo's throat.

Knowing that Samson could squeeze the breath out of him as easily as a child could wring out a wet rag, Fargo lowered his head, stretched his neck, and sank his teeth into the calf of Samson's leg.

The fabric of Samson's pants was none too clean. Fargo could taste dust and dirt, along with a little grease, but he bit down hard, trying to bite right through the cloth and make his teeth meet in the flesh of Samson's calf.

Samson growled like a grizzly and kicked back at Fargo's head with the heel of his opposite foot. He connected, and pain shot through Fargo's skull, but the Trailsman's jaws didn't relax their hold.

Samson tried another kick, but this time Fargo was ready for him. While Samson was on one leg and slightly off balance, Fargo opened his mouth, grabbed the heel of Samson's boot, and twisted.

As Samson fell, Fargo stood up, holding onto Samson's foot. Samson kicked out at him with his other leg, but Fargo twisted the foot and landed his own kick in Samson's ribs. It was like kicking the side of a barn, but Fargo did it again anyway while twisting harder on the foot, as if he were trying to twist it off the leg at the ankle.

Each time he kicked the pain in his head reminded him of the whack Prue had given him. He hoped he wasn't going to pass out. If he did, Samson would surely finish him. He kicked Samson again.

The blows weren't having much of an effect, and neither was the twisting. Samson was just too big and too strong. Fargo needed his pistol, but there was no way he was going to be able to get to it.

He'd have to use the knife.

But Samson wasn't just strong. He was also quick. In the fraction of a second it took Fargo to let go of his foot and pull the Arkansas toothpick, Samson leaped to his feet and grabbed the chair that had fallen from the loft.

Fargo had the knife out, but Samson had the chair. They stood facing each other, both out of breath, both wary and looking for an advantage.

"Nobody's ever whipped me, Fargo," Samson said. "You wouldn't have got this far if you hadn't cheated."

He feinted with the chair, but Fargo wasn't fooled. He jumped backward, ready to use the knife at the first chance he got.

"I didn't cheat," he said.

"Threw a quilt on me, by God. Got loose

from the chain again. I'd call that cheatin'."

"Better than having you kill me."

Fargo moved backward to the table.

"You can't get away from me," Samson told him. "You can't get out of this cabin."

"I'm not so sure about that," Fargo said.

He didn't take his eyes off Samson, but he did lay his knife on the table.

Samson looked puzzled, as if he suspected Fargo of some trick. The Trailsman didn't say anything. He just stood there, staring back at Samson.

"What are you up to?" Samson said.

"Nothing. I'm just tired of messing with you."

"You're just going to stand there?"

"For a while."

Samson bellowed like an enraged moose and charged, holding the chair in front of him.

He was big, and he was quick, but Fargo thought he was clumsy. He'd fought the quilt like it was alive, and he'd fallen from the loft, after all.

As soon as Samson got close, Fargo jumped to the side, grabbing one of the chairs at the table. Samson didn't change direction in time. He ran into the table, pushing it forward, and Fargo slammed the chair he was holding into the back of

Samson's head.

Fargo's blow added to the big man's momentum. The table, Samson, and Samson's chair crashed into the opposite wall. Fargo helped them all along with another solid smash to the back of Samson's head.

All the punishment finally got the better of Samson, who lay in the wreckage, unmoving. Fargo didn't think anyone would be eating off that table again anytime soon. Probably not ever. It didn't look as if it could be repaired.

The Trailsman went to stand over Samson. He bent down and made sure Samson was breathing. He was, so Fargo picked up his knife. He located his pistol, stuck it in its holster, and went up into the loft to fetch the chain and padlocks.

He wrapped them around his shoulder and climbed down. Samson still lay on the floor, so Fargo encircled him with a couple of turns of the chain and fastened it around him with the padlocks. Fargo pulled the chains against the locks to make sure they were fastened.

By the time Fargo was finished, Samson was coming to. He stirred around, and when he realized his situation, he started to struggle.

"Won't do you any good," Fargo said.

"The real Samson brought down the temple, but those chains will hold you just fine, I think."

"You let me go, you son of a bitch."

"I ought to burn down this cabin with you in it," Fargo said. "A man that would send his daughters out to die doesn't deserve any better."

"They're not going to die, you bastard."

"Maybe not," Fargo said. "Not if I can help it, anyway."

He went into Samson's bedroom and came out with his Henry. Giving Samson one more look, he went out the door, leaving Samson enchained.

22

Dobkins was satisfied that things were going along fine now. The original plan had been a good one, and he hadn't liked to abandon it, but the new one would serve.

Dobkins and Fowler were in the big coach as it rocked along the trail, swaying in the thoroughbraces. The leather curtains were open, letting in light and air. It was just as well that it had rained the night before, Dobkins thought. There wasn't any dust, and the curtains wouldn't have kept it out even if they'd been closed.

"You think this is gonna go all right?" Fowler said.

"Certainly," Dobkins said. "What could go wrong?"

"Those robbers might not show up, for one thing."

"I'm sure they were told of the shipment by that woman in the saloon. Stop worrying about it."

Fowler wasn't finished. "What about Fargo? What if he really is part of the gang?"

"All the better. We'll kill him and leave his body behind just as we'd planned to do all along. It would be perfect if he did show up."

"He's a hard man to kill, from what I've heard."

"That didn't bother you before. It shouldn't bother you now."

Fowler sat quietly for a while after that, only grunting occasionally when he bounced against the side of the coach as one of the wheels went into a shallow hole.

Finally he spoke again. "Which one are you killin', the driver or the guard?"

"I'll take the guard," Dobkins said, "but remember that we're not doing away with them until they've helped us dispose of the robbers."

"You thinkin' you'll back-shoot 'em, I reckon."

"That's an unpleasant topic, Fowler. I'd prefer not to discuss it."

"You're gonna do it, sure as hell. Why can't you talk about it?"

Dobkins preferred to ignore that remark. He thought of himself as a civilized man who occasionally had to do things that were a bit outside the law, possibly a bit outside of any mode of civilized conduct. He did such things because he had to, however, not because he enjoyed doing them. He couldn't expect a ruffian like Fowler to understand that.

Besides, getting killed while protecting the gold shipment would probably be the best thing that ever happened to the two men sitting up on top of the stage. After it was all over, Dobkins would tell a story that would make them seem like heroes, and their names would be prominently featured in newspapers all over the West. Even back east, most likely. It was a better fate than most men could ever hope for.

"We won't shoot them in the back if we can avoid it," Dobkins said. "That wouldn't look good. They're supposed to be killed by the bandits. If we have to shoot them in the back, we will, but otherwise we need to make it look good."

"If you say so."

"I do say so."

Fowler shrugged. "How long till we get stopped, do you reckon?"

Dobkins took out a heavy gold pocket watch and opened its cover. They'd been traveling for a little more than half an hour.

"Not long now," he said, snapping the watch shut. "We'll be at the next stage station if they don't hurry up and do something."

Fowler checked his Henry rifle. "I'm ready. I wish they'd do something and get it over with."

Dobkins found himself thinking the same thing. His palms were sweaty with anticipation. Not nervousness, he told himself. He never got nervous. He was simply eager for the action to begin.

And then it did. Above the creaking and rattling of the coach came a cry from above, and the stage began to slow as the driver hauled back on the reins.

Dobkins stuck his head out the window and peered down the side of the coach. A wagon was parked sideways across the road ahead, but there was no driver. No one was in sight. No horse was hitched to the wagon.

"It's a trap," Dobkins called up to Avinger. "The best thing would be to start shooting as soon as anybody shows himself."

"Don't see anybody," Avinger said as the coach drew to a halt.

Dobkins opened the door and stepped out of the coach, his shotgun at the ready. On the other side, Fowler got out with his Henry.

It was quiet, and Dobkins studied the rocks on either side of the trail. The wagon was conveniently located so that anyone who'd been in it would have a place to hide. The rocks also prevented the coach from pulling around the wagon and continuing on its way.

Dobkins hugged the side of the coach, waiting, watching, and wondering what would happen next.

"What do you think?" the driver asked Avinger.

"I think somebody wants me or you to move that wagon. Might be better if one of our passengers did it, though."

Fowler looked at Dobkins through the windows of the coach. Dobkins shook his head.

"No," he said. "Moving it's up to you if you want to do it. I think we should wait."

"Can't wait all day," the driver said. "I got a schedule to keep, and I gotta drive the stage."

"All right, dammit," Avinger said. "I'll move the blasted wagon."

He climbed down, holding his shotgun, and started toward the wagon. He looked from side to side as he walked.

Dobkins was doing more listening than looking. If someone were hiding in the rocks, he'd have to come out sooner or later if his plan was to rob the stage.

When that happened, Dobkins would shoot whoever it was. That would bring the odds down, making them four against three, assuming that the usual four owlhoots were out there. Dobkins always liked to improve the odds.

A horse whinnied from behind the rocks, and a robber stepped out into the road.

Dobkins pulled the trigger of the shotgun before he had a chance to speak.

Fargo found his saddle easily enough, and soon the Ovaro was saddled and the Trailsman was on his way. The mud flew from beneath the big stallion's hooves, and Fargo hoped he'd be in time to stop whatever it was that Prue was dreading.

He could have used Samson's help, but he hadn't wanted to take any chances with him. Samson wouldn't listen to reason, especially not as angry as he was at being whipped by the Trailsman.

However, Fargo had deliberately left Samson a bit of an opportunity, if the big man had enough sense to take advantage of it.

Even if he had enough sense to take advantage of it, he might not figure out what to do next. That was up to him. His thinking didn't run in the same direction that a normal man's might.

Fargo could understand why Samson wanted revenge on Ferriday, but he couldn't figure why he'd use his daughters to get it. It would make a lot more sense to Fargo to make a trip to Saint Jo and beat the living hell out of Ferriday, and let it go at that. Samson didn't think that way, though, not that Fargo could tell.

And then there was the business of not killing anybody. No doubt the sisters had something to do with that idea, but Samson didn't hold with killing, either. It seemed to Fargo that a man bent on revenge wouldn't care how he got it, but not Samson. He had to do things differently.

It was a mystery, and Fargo didn't think he was the man to solve it. All he wanted to do was to get to the trail before something terrible happened to the sisters.

However, there was another mystery that bothered Fargo.

The gold shipment.

Why was Ferriday hauling it? He'd made a policy of avoiding shipments like that because of the danger involved. Carrying gold was asking for trouble.

Maybe Ferriday thought that, since his stage was getting robbed for small things, he might as well go ahead and take the risk of running a big shipment through, but that wasn't likely. A businessman didn't think that way, or at least no businessman that Fargo had ever known.

The Trailsman found he couldn't think like either Ferriday or Samson, even though both of them were mixed up in this mess together.

Fargo got the feeling that there were things going on he didn't know about, and that somehow Prue was right about his part in the robbery, even if he didn't know what that part was. For that matter, Prue didn't know herself.

Fargo had known Indians who had some kind of second sight, who could foretell events or sense things that were beyond the understanding of most folks, but he'd never known a white woman like that. Prue could do it, though. He'd seen enough evidence of it to believe.

Which got him to wondering why she'd gone along with her sisters so uncomplainingly. If she knew there was a disaster waiting for them, why not just refuse to go?

Samson wouldn't have stood for it, Fargo supposed, but the sisters all together might have been able to persuade him that he was wrong.

There was no use to worry about any of it. Fargo shook his aching head to clear it and urged the Ovaro on.

Fargo hadn't been gone long before Samson figured out that there was a little slack in the chains that bound him. He thought he could wiggle out of them if he could concentrate and be careful.

Concentration and care were two things that were pretty much foreign to him, but if he wanted to get loose, he'd have to be more disciplined than usual.

It was pretty stupid of that bastard Fargo to have left him a way out, Samson thought as he worked his body like a snake, trying to shed the chains like a rattler sheds its skin.

After only a few minutes the chains had slipped down over Samson's hands, and he was able to push them the rest of the way off. He stood up, shook himself, and realized that his ribs were sore.

That damned Fargo had hurt him. It had been a long time since Samson had been hurt by anybody in a fight, not since prison, in fact. Fargo would have to pay for that, but he'd run off like a coward.

So Samson would have to go after him. When he caught up with him, he wouldn't shoot him. He'd break his neck instead. That seemed like a fair exchange.

While he was saddling his horse, Samson realized that he was still thinking about killing Fargo. It was wrong to do that for revenge. He'd been willing to do it while Fargo was a danger to him, but now Fargo had gotten away. If he was planning to tell the soldiers or some U.S. Marshal about Samson, it was probably too late to do anything about it unless Samson could catch up to him and stop him. He might have to kill him to stop him. That would make it all right.

The Ovaro was a good-looking horse, and Fargo wasn't nearly as heavy as Samson, so Samson thought there wasn't much chance of catching up.

But he knew he'd have to try.

23

The four sisters hadn't been happy about things when they left the cabin. They hadn't said anything to Samson, but as they rode toward the trail they argued about Prue's premonition and what it might mean.

"We could always turn back," Hope said. "We could tell Father that we missed the stage."

"He'd never believe that," Faith told her. "He knows the schedule as well as we do."

Prue drove the wagon, the reins held loosely in her fingers. She said, "We have to go through with it. There's nothing we can do to change things."

Hope shivered. "I wish I knew where you get those feelings of yours, Prue. I wish they didn't always turn out to be true."

"They don't, not always. Sometimes things don't happen the way I feel they will. Fargo could have changed this one."

Charity didn't agree. "I still don't see what

he has to do with it."

"I don't either," Prue said. "But he does."

They went along in silence for a while, and then Prue spoke up again.

"There's one thing we can do that might make a difference," she said. "If everyone will agree."

"Tell us what it is first," Charity said.

"You have to let me play your part."

"No. I'm always the one who takes the lead."

The wagon wheels creaked. A hawk flew across the blue sky on his way to parts unknown.

"That's why I have to take over," Prue said. "We have to do things different from the way we've always done them. If we change our plan, we can change what happens."

They wrangled about that for a while, but Prue didn't join in. She had a feeling about what would happen if they changed the plan. It wouldn't be good for her, but it would probably save Charity's life.

"Will it make things better?" Charity asked.

"I'd say so," Prue said, because that was what she thought Charity needed to hear.

And it was true in a way. Prue believed the other two needed Charity more than they needed her. Charity stood up to their father more than Prue ever did.

"If it will make things better, we should do it," Hope said. "Don't you think so, Faith?"

Faith agreed, but Charity wasn't persuaded so easily. "What if you're wrong this time?" she said.

"I could be wrong," Prue said.

"You never are," Faith said.

Prue just shrugged and let her sisters do the talking. There was some more argument, but in the end Prue got her way. When they arrived at the spot where they planned to stop the stage, Prue located the wagon in the middle of the trail. They unhitched the horse and led it behind the rocks.

"Are we going to get the gold?" Charity asked her before they pulled their handkerchiefs up to cover the lower halves of their faces. "What does your feeling tell you?"

"I'm not sure about that," Prue said. "I don't think we'll get it, though."

"Then why are we going through with this?"

"You know why. We're doing it for the same reason we always do. Because it's what Father wants."

Charity sighed. "You're right. Are we going to live through it?"

"We should," Prue said, her voice low.

Charity reached out to touch her shoulder. "Are you sure about that?"

"Almost," Prue said.

She was sure about the others, though she wasn't at all sure about herself.

"Then I guess we have to go through with it," Charity said, dropping her hand. "Sometimes I think we should start living for ourselves and let Father get his own revenge."

"After this, maybe we should," Prue said, hoping there would be an *after.*

Faith and Hope had joined them for the last part of the conversation.

"Who's going to tell Father if we decide to stop?" Hope asked.

"I will," Prue said. To herself she added, "If I live through this."

"We'll let you," Faith said with a short laugh.

"And if you won't, I will," Charity said. "Now let's get ready to rob the stage."

As soon as the robber moved into sight, Dobkins' shotgun roared.

Avinger hit the ground. The bandit fell backward, landing at the side of the road near the rear of the wagon.

"What the hell!" the driver shouted, and

the Henry boomed, chipping off a chunk of a big rock just above the fallen bandit's head.

Someone reached out and took hold of the wounded owlhoot's shoulders, dragging the body behind the rocks.

"Shit," the driver said.

Avinger slithered like a snake and went off into the rocks before Dobkins could get off his second shot.

"This is like a damn war," the driver said. "What are you two doing?"

"Missed the son of a bitch," Fowler said. "What do we do now?"

There was no movement behind the rocks, no response from the robbers. Dobkins wondered where the hell Avinger had gone. Maybe he was sneaking up on the robbers right now. That was it. Had to be. Avinger was a company man all the way, and he wouldn't have any regard for the risk involved with four against one.

Dobkins walked around behind the coach and came up to Fowler.

"What now?" Fowler said.

"Somebody has to go after them and help Avinger," Dobkins said.

The driver must have overheard them. He said, "It ain't gonna be me. I'm just the driver. Avinger's the guard, and you two said you were going to help. I'd say Avinger's the one who needs help about now."

"I'm not going after him," Fowler said. He gave a glance up toward the driver. "I'll take care of my part of this, but that's all."

If the driver knew what Fowler meant by his last remark, he gave no sign.

"Fine," Dobkins told Fowler. "You stay here and watch those rocks. I'll see about Avinger."

He tried to sound as if he knew what he was doing, but he didn't. He'd spent most of his life in cities and towns, and he didn't like the idea of going into those rocks one bit. He supposed he had to, however.

If things went well, he and Avinger could drive the bandits away, and they'd leave the one Dobkins had shot behind. Then Dobkins would dispose of Avinger while Fowler eliminated the driver. What could go wrong?

He smiled, broke his shotgun, and flicked out the spent cartridge, replacing it with another.

"We're getting out of here," Charity said after she had pulled Prue to safety.

"What about the gold?" Faith said.

"To hell with the gold. It's Prue that matters now."

"Is she alive?" Faith said, staring down at her sister.

Prue didn't look good. The shotgun pellets had spread and struck her in the face and side. What could be seen of her face was bruised and bloody, and blood stained her clothing.

"She's alive for now," Charity said. "And I'm not staying here until she dies or the rest of us get killed. I don't think the gold is worth it. Father wouldn't think so, either."

Faith wasn't so sure of that, but she agreed with her sister about leaving.

So did Hope, who said, "We need the wagon."

"We can't hitch up the horse," Charity said. "Prue will have to ride with one of us."

"She won't be able to hang on."

"We'll tie her to the spare horse," Charity said. "Let's do it and get out of here."

They worked fast and were almost done when they saw Fargo riding toward them.

"How did he get away?" Hope said.

"I don't know," Charity said. "Ride out and warn him. We'll finish up here."

Hope got on her horse and went to warn Fargo.

Dobkins saw Avinger in the rocks ahead.

"Avinger," he whispered. "It's me,

Dobkins."

Avinger glanced around and signaled for Dobkins to join him. Dobkins was apprehensive, but he moved forward just the same. When he got to Avinger's side, the guard pointed for him to take a look past the rock that sheltered them.

Dobkins hesitated, and Avinger gave him a nudge with his elbow. Dobkins looked. He saw two of the robbers tying their wounded friend to a horse, while a third rode away toward someone who seemed on his way to join them.

Dobkins didn't know who the rider was, but he didn't like the idea of a fifth man coming along. He could easily kill one of the others now. He raised his shotgun to fire.

Avinger reached out and shoved his gun barrel down.

"No use in killin' 'em," he said, keeping his voice low. "Let 'em leave. It don't matter if they get away. We ain't lawmen, and it ain't our job to catch 'em. We still got the gold. That's all we care about."

Dobkins thought it was about time to get rid of Avinger, which is what he would have done right then if he hadn't been careless. One of the robbers had seen him and fired off a shot at him.

The bullet pinged off the rock, and Dobkins dived to shelter. Things weren't going at all the way he'd thought they would.

"We'd better fight back," he said.

Avinger took a quick look over the rock and shook his head. "Nope. Looks like they're leaving. We'll let 'em go."

That would never do. Dobkins had to have a body. He stood up, stepped out, and fired at the retreating riders.

They had already gotten too far for the shotgun to be effective, but the pellets had enough force to carry them into the rump of the trailing horse.

The horse jumped wildly and threw its rider. Dobkins wasn't overly familiar with shotguns. He thought the rider was dead, which was all he'd hoped for. The others could keep right on going.

Well, one body, not counting the guard and the driver.

Dobkins turned and shot Avinger full in the face.

24

Fargo saw the rider fall and didn't stop to greet Hope or the others. He rode to where Faith was trying to get to her feet. When he reached her, he took her hand and pulled her up behind him on the Ovaro, then wheeled the big horse around and headed back the way he'd come.

He and Faith caught up with the others easily enough, well out of range of the shotgun.

"Time for you to get out of here," Fargo told them. "If you meet Samson, tell him to keep on coming."

Faith climbed from the Ovaro's back to sit behind Charity.

"How did you get away?" Charity said.

"Later," Fargo told her. "What happened back there?"

"They tried to kill us," Charity said. "We didn't get a chance to say a word."

"I'll try to set things straight," Fargo said,

wondering just how he'd manage to do that.

"They aren't asking questions," Hope said. "They're just shooting, and they might shoot you."

"I'll take the chance," Fargo said. "Get back to the cabin."

They didn't argue about it. When they were on their way, Fargo started for the stage.

Dobkins had been a little sickened by what he'd done to Avinger. He hadn't expected it to be quite so messy. Quite a bit of Avinger was stuck to the rock that had been behind him. The rest lay on the ground.

It had to be done, Dobkins told himself. It was just a part of getting the gold.

When Dobkins got back to the stage, the driver asked what had happened.

"The bastards killed Avinger," Dobkins said, looking at Fowler.

Fowler stepped around to the front of the stage and raised the Henry.

"Put that thing down," the driver said, just before Fowler shot him right in the brisket.

The driver pitched out of the box, dead before he hit the ground. Fowler didn't seem bothered by what he'd done, and Dobkins didn't look at the body.

"What next?" Fowler said.

"We hide the gold," Dobkins told him. "Then we go back to Laramie and report what happened."

"Looks like we might have company first," Fowler said, pointing the barrel of the Henry toward the approaching rider.

"Shit," Dobkins said. "Kill him."

"Who is it?"

"Does it matter?"

"I guess not," Fowler said.

Fargo couldn't figure out what was happening, but he knew it wasn't right. One of the two men still with the stage had shot the driver, and now it looked like he was going to shoot Fargo as well.

Fargo pulled up on the reins and jumped off the Ovaro, hitting the ground and rolling behind a rock.

Not far away from him lay the body of Avinger, obviously killed by a shotgun blast. None of the sisters would have killed him. Fargo was certain of that. So what was going on?

A bullet ricocheted off the rock in front of him. Whatever was happening, it was clear that Fargo didn't have any friends on the stage and that it wasn't going to be easy to straighten things out.

He'd thought that, once the women were

gone, it would be easy enough to explain to the stage guards that he was in Ferriday's employ, that he'd come to Laramie to prevent robberies, and that it was safe for the stage to go on its way.

Now the driver and one of the guards were dead, and it looked like the other two were out to kill him just as they'd killed the driver and the guard.

Which meant that the men weren't guards, after all. They were after the gold, just like the sisters had been.

Well, Fargo had been sent to prevent robberies, and that's what he intended to do, if he could.

When he looked around the rock, the two men were sitting in the box. One of them was driving and had eased the stage back to a place where it could get off the trail and try to get around the rocks on the side opposite from where Fargo was. The terrain was pretty rough, and the going wouldn't be easy, but they might make it. And then they'd get away if Fargo didn't stop them.

He figured he'd better do that.

When Fargo mounted the Ovaro and started after the stage, Dobkins recognized him.

"Where the hell did *he* come from?" Dobkins asked.

"Who is it?" Fowler wanted to know. He had all he could do to drive the stage and couldn't look around.

"It's Fargo. We can't let him catch us."

"I don't know how the hell you plan to stop him."

The stage lurched, and Dobkins nearly fell off. He grabbed the rail and hung on. He knew he couldn't shoot anyone from where he was sitting. He wouldn't be able to hold the gun steady.

"We'll have to outrun him," he told Fowler.

Fowler shook his head. "Can't do it." He bounced up about a foot as the stage hit a bump. "Too rough."

"You have to try. We have a good start on him. Get back on the trail. It'll smooth out."

They were around the rocks, and Fowler pulled the reins to the right. The team responded, and the stage lurched hard again and tilted hard to the left. For a second Dobkins thought it would fall over, but it bounced back upright. Then they were on the trail, and the going was much smoother.

"He'll never catch us now," Dobkins said, but it wasn't long before he knew he was wrong. The big Ovaro was slowly gaining ground.

The only good thing Dobkins could think

of was that Fargo couldn't do any better shooting at him than he could by shooting at Fargo. Dobkins figured Fargo wouldn't be able to do much to stop them even if he caught the coach, so he urged Fowler to keep going.

"Faster, if you can," he added.

"We can't go any faster," Fowler said. "You wanta try drivin'?"

Dobkins didn't bother to answer.

"If he gets too close," Fowler said, "use that scattergun of yours. You won't have to be too steady with it. Even if you don't kill him, some of the shot's bound to hit him. Maybe you can knock him off that horse."

Dobkins figured that advice was as good as any. He got the shotgun and turned to look back. "Shit," he said.

"What now?" Fowler said.

"There's somebody else coming after us."

Dobkins watched the man riding along the trail behind Fargo. He was a good ways back, and he was even bigger than the Trailsman.

"Maybe he's after Fargo," Fowler said.

Dobkins hoped so. He didn't want to have to deal with both of them. But if the shotgun would handle one, it would handle the other, too. Let them get close enough, and

Dobkins wouldn't mind pulling the trigger at all. It wouldn't be messy, the way it had been with Avinger.

In fact, Dobkins looked forward to it.

Fargo knew he was going to catch up to the stagecoach. It was just a matter of time. What he didn't know was what he'd do when he got there. One of the men had a shotgun, and that was a dangerous proposition.

There was something familiar about the man, and Fargo squinted his eyes. Damn if it wasn't Ferriday's man. Dobkins. He wasn't wearing his dude clothes, but it was Dobkins all right. Fargo wouldn't have figured the little man for a thief, but he was taking the gold, all right. He would have known about the shipment, being in Ferriday's employ and trusted with the boss' secrets, and he must have decided it would be worth the risk to steal it.

Fargo heard something behind him and took a quick gander. He saw Samson and grinned. The big man had figured out how to get out of the chains that Fargo had deliberately left a little loose.

Fargo didn't know if the women had met Samson and told him what had happened or not. If they had, Samson might not be as angry at Fargo as he would have been under other circumstances. He'd want the men who'd shot his daughter more than he wanted Fargo, and those men were on the stage.

Fargo couldn't afford to slow down. Samson would just have to catch up if he was able.

As he got nearer to the coach, Fargo stayed right in the middle of the trail. He didn't want to give Dobkins a shot at him with the scattergun. If Dobkins wanted to shoot, he'd have to turn around, and if he tried that, he'd probably fall off. Or he could climb on top of the swaying stage, and if he tried that, he was likely to go flying over the side. Fargo didn't think Dobkins would take that chance.

Mud whirled up from under the coach's wheels and spun in Fargo's direction. He looked at the leather boot on the back of the coach. He knew that the gold would be inside it. All he had to do was get to it.

He found himself dodging mud as he came right up to the rear of the coach. He stayed to the driver's side so Dobkins couldn't lean around and take a shot at him, though he didn't think there was much chance of that.

A short rail ran from the top of the coach

about a quarter of the way down the boot. Fargo turned in the saddle and reached out with his right hand to grab it. The Ovaro slowed, and Fargo was pulled free of the saddle. The Ovaro ran off the trail as Fargo swung up onto the boot.

He had to cling to the rail with all the strength of his arm and hand to avoid being thrown free of the stage. With his free right hand he pulled the Arkansas toothpick and sliced through the leather cover of the boot, cutting a sizeable opening.

Inside the boot were the mail sacks and several small wooden boxes. Fargo knew they must hold the gold.

Fargo looked back down the trail. Samson was coming along as fast as he could, but he was mighty big, and his horse was tiring. He wasn't going to be able to catch the stage unless it came to a halt.

Fargo thought he'd give Samson something to look at, maybe even stop for. He stepped into the opening he'd cut and braced himself as best he could in the rocking compartment. It was cramped, but he still found a way to spread his legs and sheathe his knife. He bent down to reach one of the boxes.

The lid of the box was nailed tight. Fargo took hold of the box and tumbled it out of the boot. It landed on the trail and broke open. Gold bars glittered in the sun.

25

"The son of a bitch is throwing out the gold," Dobkins said. "Stop the coach."

Fowler pulled on the brake handle, and the coach began to slow.

Dobkins pulled himself up onto the roof of the coach. Lying on his stomach, he inched toward the rear, holding the shotgun in one hand.

Fargo heard the squeal of the brake and sensed the slowing of the coach. He looked back down the trail to see if Samson had reached the gold. He had, and he stopped to look at it. He didn't dismount, however. He gave the gold a cursory glance and started after the coach again. Fargo didn't know if that was good or bad, or if it meant anything at all.

He heard something scrape on the coach roof and figured someone was coming after him, probably Dobkins. He pulled his big .45 and waited for Dobkins to stick his head over the rail at the back of the roof. If the head appeared, Fargo planned to put a hole in it.

The coach slowed to a stop and Dobkins still hadn't shown up. A minute passed, then two. Dobkins must have been working up his nerve.

Samson was getting closer to them. Dobkins probably didn't like the idea of taking on two men, Fargo thought, and then he saw the barrel of the shotgun poke past the edge of the roof, pointing at Samson.

Fargo reached to take hold of the barrel and pull the gun away from Dobkins. Just when his fingers closed around the barrel, the gun went off.

Fargo was so surprised that he fell backward out of the boot and onto his back on the muddy trail.

Samson tumbled off his horse at the same moment, as the buckshot plowed into him.

Fargo hadn't dropped his pistol. He looked up just in time to see Dobkins standing on top of the coach, staring down at him over the barrel of the shotgun. Fargo flipped up the .45 and pulled the trigger.

He had no time to aim, but his bullet hit Dobkins anyway. The little man threw the shotgun into the air and fell off the coach.

The shotgun hit the coach roof, bounced, and slid over the side.

Fargo stood up. Dobkins was alive. He twitched on the ground, and the coach started to pull away. The driver didn't care enough about Dobkins to stick around, and Fargo was only just able to grab hold of the boot and pull himself inside before the stage escaped him.

The fall had knocked the wind out of him, so he bounced around in the boot for a minute, holding to the side rails until his breathing returned to normal. When it did, he looked to see what had become of Samson.

It appeared that he wasn't dead. He was standing up, staring at the retreating coach.

Fargo would have to deal with him later. At the moment he had other things to do. He stood up and took hold of the top rail, then pulled himself up and onto the roof. He could see the driver's back as the man leaned forward to urge the horses on.

Fargo was no better at crossing the roof than Dobkins would have been, but it was a much shorter trip for him because he was so much taller than Dobkins. In fact, when he lay flat and stretched out, he was as long as the coach.

He put the barrel of his pistol to the back

of the driver's head. "Stop the coach," he said.

Fowler didn't flinch. He didn't reach for the brake, either. "I ain't stoppin'," he said. "Shoot me if you want to, but then you'll have to do the drivin'."

Fargo didn't want to shoot him, so he tapped him on the side of the head with the gun barrel. Not too gently.

Fowler turned angrily and spat a curse at Fargo.

Fargo tapped him on the forehead with the pistol barrel.

"Stop the coach," Fargo said, but Fowler didn't.

Instead he threw himself forward, onto the back of one of the horses in the team. Fargo was so surprised that he didn't know for a second what to do.

The delay gave Fowler time for one more move. He was still holding the reins. He tossed them forward and jumped off the horse, landing on his shoulder and rolling across the ground, leaving Fargo on top of the stage with the horses running free.

Samson wasn't hurt too much, though the places where the buckshot had hit him stung, and some of them were bleeding. He knew he looked like hell, but he wasn't hit as badly as Prue had been, and he figured the son of a bitch who'd put the buckshot in him was the same one who'd shot Prue.

Samson didn't even bother to get back on his horse. He shambled forward, toward the man Fargo had shot. Samson wanted to make damn sure the son of a bitch was dead; and if he wasn't, well, Samson would finish the job.

Dobkins still lay on the ground when Samson got to him. He was shot in the chest, still twitching, and Samson could hear him breathing with a wet, whistling sound. He kicked him in the foot.

"What's your name?" he said.

Dobkins didn't answer except to take another breath that whistled in his chest.

Lung shot, Samson thought. Poor bastard. He was gonna do some suffering before he died, and even if he had shot Prue, not to mention Samson, it was a fate the big man wouldn't have wished on him.

"Why'd you shoot my daughter?" Samson said, not really expecting an answer, and of course he didn't get one, though Dobkins' eyes did flutter open.

"Fargo's the one shot you," Samson said. "Not me, not that it matters a whole hell of a lot."

"Fargo," Dobkins said, or that's what

Samson thought he heard. It was hard to tell because of the blood that gushed out of Dobkins' mouth when he tried to speak.

"Messed us up," Dobkins said, or something like that. Samson wasn't sure.

"Fargo's good at messing folks up," Samson said. "Right now he's messing up your partner."

Whether Dobkins heard or not, Samson didn't know. Dobkins closed his eyes and lay still, but the whistling sound continued. Dobkins was drowning in his own blood, and there wasn't much Samson could do for him.

And since Dobkins had shot him, and probably Prue as well, Samson didn't think he'd do anything even if he could.

Samson thought about the gold, and he thought about his daughters. He could have the gold if he wanted it, or some of it. It was just lying back there in the road, easy pickings, but for some reason Samson found he didn't even care about it. He'd risked his daughters' lives for it, and he realized now that he'd been wrong all along, about a lot of things. The girls should never have been his instruments of vengeance, though he had justified that by telling himself it was their vengeance as well. He'd lost a wife and had plenty of reason to grieve and want revenge, but she'd been their mother, after all. He'd thought they had an obligation.

The thing was, they didn't feel the way he did. They missed their mother, but they knew that getting revenge on Ferriday wouldn't bring her back.

What they wanted was to get on with their lives, maybe have families of their own, and he should have let them do that instead of using them for his own purposes.

Maybe it wasn't too late to change things, he thought. Maybe, if he was lucky, he could even get on with his own life.

His horse had followed him to where Dobkins lay. It nudged him in the back, and Samson said, "I guess I'll go see what I can do to help Fargo."

He saw the shotgun lying not far from Dobkins and went to get it. He checked the loads and found that only one cartridge had been fired. That left him one for somebody else.

Samson climbed on his horse. It wasn't too painful. When he was mounted, he looked down at Dobkins. Still breathing, but the whistling wasn't as loud.

Samson rode off and left him to his dying.

Fargo didn't have much choice. He could try using the brake, but he didn't think that alone would stop a headlong coach and a fast-moving team of horses. The best bet would be to use the reins.

So he leaped from the box onto the back of the horse in front of him. He clamped his legs around the horse and clung to its mane until he was sure he wasn't going to fall off.

The reins were dragging and bouncing along the ground below the pole and the whippletree. Fargo tightened his grip on the horse's mane with his left hand and leaned as far as he could to the right. He smelled wet earth and horseflesh as bits of mud smacked into him. The sound of the hooves beating the ground and the creaking of the traces and tugs was loud in his ears. If the pole moved to the side and hit his head, he was a goner for sure, he thought as he swung down, his fingers reaching for the reins.

He almost had them twice, but missed. Then a lucky bounce brought them up just as he grabbed, and he shut his hand on them and sat up.

There wasn't a chance he could get back to the seat and apply the brake, so he heaved back on the reins. The horses resisted for a few seconds, but then the coach began to slow down. After a while it came to a stop.

Fargo sat still for a while, the horse

breathing heavily beneath him. The Ovaro had followed along for a short distance, but had veered off the road and stopped. He was grazing on the sparse grass beside the trail, about halfway to where the driver of the stage was now standing.

When Fargo jumped to the ground, he saw that Samson had stopped to have a talk with the driver. The Trailsman wondered what they were saying. He had a feeling that Samson wasn't just passing the time of day.

He was right.

26

Fowler hadn't taken the Henry with him when he jumped from the stage, but he still had his pistol. He pulled it and had it pointing at Samson long before he got there.

"You don't look so good," Fowler said when Samson reined up about twenty yards away.

Samson knew he didn't look good, what with all those shotgun pellets in him; but he didn't care. He felt a little like bees were stinging him, nothing to bother him much. He could still walk and ride.

"Who are you?" he asked Fowler.

"None of your damn business." Fowler waggled the pistol, but the barrel didn't move very far. "Why don't you get down off that horse?"

"Why should I?"

"Because I'm the one needs a ride. You can meet up with your friend and ride on the stage."

"I like my horse better," Samson said.

"Then I'll have to kill you, because I'm leavin' before Fargo gets here."

Samson shook his head. "If you're gonna put it that way, I'll get down."

As he started to dismount, he turned his horse's head slightly so the animal moved between him and Fowler. He came out of the saddle on the side of the horse opposite Fowler, and when his feet touched the ground, he dropped down, drawing his pistol, turning, and firing between the horse's legs.

The horse leaped away, and the bullet took Fowler in the foot.

Fowler howled with pain and dropped to his knees, but he got off a shot as he fell. The bullet buzzed by Samson's head, and the big man shot Fowler twice, once in the face and once in the heart. Either one would have done the job, but Samson had been in a hurry.

Fowler remained in place on his knees for a couple of seconds. Then his pistol fell from his fingers and he toppled forward onto what was left of his face.

Samson stood and waited for Fargo to get there.

"Looks like we've about wiped 'em out,"

Samson said when Fargo rode up. "You got one, and I got one."

"They got the driver and the guard," Fargo said. "You look like hell."

"People keep tellin' me that. I reckon I'll live."

Fargo said he reckoned the same. "You planning to shoot me, or are you just holding onto that pistol for comfort?"

Samson raised the pistol and looked at it. He stuck it in the holster and said, "I forgot I was holdin' it. I was all wrong about you, Fargo. I don't think I want to shoot you anymore."

That was fine with the Trailsman, but he wanted to know why Samson had changed his mind.

"Mainly because I figure it was these two fellas we killed that shot Prue. You came to help 'em, accordin' to what the girls told me. I wouldn't listen to Prue when she had misgivin's, but you did. I guess I owe you now."

"You don't owe me anything."

"That may be your thinkin'. It's not mine." Samson looked down at Fowler. "Lots of dead folks around here. What are we gonna do about this mess?"

"That's kind of up to you," Fargo said.

Samson glanced back at Fargo. "Up to

me? How's that?"

"Well, first of all there's the gold. You saw some of it lying in the road back there. You still want it?"

Samson shook his head. "I was wrong about that. Takin' that gold would hurt Ferriday's business, maybe, but it would hurt somebody else worse, whoever it belonged to. It's like to have got my girls killed already, at least one of 'em, anyway. I should've listened to Prue. I should've listened to you when you tried to warn me."

Fargo was glad to see that Samson had come around to his way of thinking. He'd have hated to have to shoot him, which he'd have done if Samson had given him trouble. He'd have hated to do it, not because he was so fond of Samson, but because he figured he owed it to the big man's daughters to keep their father alive.

"I'm givin' up on Ferriday," Samson went on. "Gettin' revenge on him was a mistake." He grinned. "I got better things to do."

"You sure you want to give it up?"

"He deserves to suffer for what he did to me, but I've been goin' about it the wrong way. You had a better idea. Anyway, I'm givin' up on the robbin'. My girls won't be ridin' out again, and I'm changin' my ways."

"Kate Follett will be glad to hear that."

"How'd you know that's what I had in mind? You got the second sight like Prue?"

"I'm nothing like Prue. I just guessed it."

"It was a good guess. What're we gonna do about all these dead folks?"

Fargo thought it over. He said, "Gather them up and take them to the fort in the coach. We'll let Colonel Alexander's soldiers bury them. Calhoun will have to see about getting another driver to carry the gold the rest of the way."

"We better pick up that gold you threw out, too."

"We will. Don't be thinking of keeping any of it."

"Hell, you don't have to worry about that."

Fargo worried just a little anyway, but Samson didn't seem interested in the gold at all. They put it in the boot and put the bodies in the coach. It was a messy job.

"Have to clean this coach before they take it on down the line," Samson said.

"Calhoun's job," Fargo said. "Not ours. Can you drive it?"

"I can handle a team, if that's what you mean."

Samson tied his horse to the rear of the coach and told Fargo they'd have to take it slow.

"We got some kind of story we're gonna tell?" he said. "Might be a good idea to have one."

Fargo had been thinking about that. He said, "We have one."

"You gonna keep me and the girls out of it?"

"They take one look at you at the fort, and they'll know you were in it."

"As long as the girls get off, I don't care. What you got in mind?"

Fargo told him.

"You're telling me these two dead men, Dobkins and the other one, were the leaders of the outlaw gang?" Colonel Alexander asked.

Samson and Fargo sat across from Alexander's desk in the colonel's office. They'd cleaned up, and the post doctor had picked the shotgun pellets out of Samson's skin, or as many of them as he could get. One or two would have to remain embedded there. Fargo hoped the same wasn't true of Prue. She'd been farther away from Dobkins when he shot her than Samson had been, so Fargo probably didn't have to worry.

"That's right," Fargo told Alexander. "Dobkins was the inside man. He worked with Ferriday in Saint Jo, and he knew what

256

the passengers were carrying. That's why the robbers hit the stage only when somebody had valuables."

Alexander didn't look convinced. "Some of those passengers boarded here. Dobkins couldn't have known about them."

Fargo was prepared for that. He said, "That's where the other fella came in. If you check around, you'll probably find out that he's been hanging around the fort for a while. He'd talk to the passengers at the stage station or in the saloon, and find out who was carrying what."

"Maybe," Alexander said. "What about the other three men?"

"Three?" Samson said, and Fargo kicked his foot. Samson didn't say any more. Fargo hoped he'd caught on to the fact that if Dobkins was in Saint Jo, he couldn't have been with the gang.

"They got away," Fargo said. "Samson was wounded, and we had our hands full with the two on the coach. It's lucky we were out there today, or they'd all have got clean away."

"Why do you think Dobkins came all the way out here for this robbery?" Alexander asked.

"He and his friend didn't want to take any chances," Fargo said. "They wanted to be sure they killed the guard and the driver. If Samson and I hadn't come along when we did, they'd have gotten the gold and blamed everything on the three who got away."

"What do you think happened to those three?"

"I think they're headed away from here as fast as they can go. I'd say you don't have to worry about them anymore, and neither does Ferriday."

"Well," Alexander said, clasping his hands and putting them in front of him on the desk, "all's well that ends well, I suppose."

"Yeah," Samson said. "That's a certain fact, Colonel, a certain fact."

When they left the office, Fargo said, "What now, Samson?"

"I gotta see about my daughters. Don't you want to ride out to the place with me and look in on Prue?"

"Yeah," Fargo said. "I do. You want to make any stops first?"

Samson mumbled something.

"What was that?" Fargo said.

"I said I might stop off at Kate's store if you weren't in a big hurry."

Fargo grinned. "I have plenty of time," he said.

Kate had already heard all about the attempted stage robbery and Samson's wounds.

"You look terrible," she said, scolding him. "You need to take better care of yourself."

"Maybe he needs someone to take care of him," Fargo said.

Both of them looked at him.

"He has his daughters," Kate said.

"They might decide to find someone else to take care of," Fargo said. "Plenty of young men with prospects posted here at the fort, and they'd all be lucky to have wives like the Coleman sisters."

Kate turned to Samson. "You have any idea what he's suggesting?"

"Well, you're a mighty handsome woman, Kate, and I was thinkin' . . ."

"You'd have to cut your hair," Kate said, cutting him off. "And find some better-looking clothes. Aside from that, maybe you have prospects yourself. If you want to come courting me, I can't say I'd object."

Fargo grinned. It looked to him like Samson was hooked and landed.

27

Two months later, Fargo found himself in Saint Jo again, sitting in Ferriday's office.

"I was wondering if I'd ever see you again, Fargo. You did a good job out there at Laramie for me, and I never got a chance to thank you."

Ferriday didn't look good, Fargo thought, not as prosperous and chipper as he'd been the last time they met. He looked sadder and older. He didn't look much like he really wanted to thank Fargo, either.

That was fine with Fargo. He hadn't come here for thanks.

"It was too bad about Dobkins," he said.

Ferriday nodded and looked even sadder. "Yes, it was. I always trusted him. It's hard to believe he'd go after that gold shipment. I should have known better than to take it."

"I was wondering why you did that."

Ferriday avoided his eyes. "I needed the money. The shipment paid well."

"You were lucky it got through."

"Thanks to you."

Ferriday sounded more bitter than grateful, Fargo thought.

"Yeah, thanks to me."

"If you're looking for more money, Fargo, you came to the wrong place," Ferriday said. "You were paid in full, in advance, and that's all the money you're going to get."

"I didn't come here for money. I didn't come to hear you thank me, either."

Ferriday got a bit agitated. "Then why in the hell *did* you come here?"

"I wanted you to meet somebody."

"Meet somebody? I don't want to meet anybody. I don't have time for any such foolishness, Fargo." Ferriday stood up. "I think it's time for you to leave. Good day to you."

Fargo stood, too. "Good day to you, too, then, but this fella I wanted you to meet's right outside. He'll be real disappointed if he doesn't see you." Fargo walked to the office door and opened it. "Come on in, Samson."

Samson loomed in the doorway. His hair was cut short, but he was wearing his old clothes. He had to duck under the lintel to get into the office.

"This is Mr. Ferriday, Samson. Mr. Ferriday, meet Samson Coleman."

"We've met already," Samson said. "I expect Mr. Ferriday remembers me pretty well."

Ferriday backed away from the desk. Fargo figured he knew who Samson was, all right.

Samson stepped forward and stuck out his hand, but Ferriday didn't move forward to shake it. He pressed against the wall, looking around as if hoping a door might suddenly open somewhere nearby.

There wasn't a door, however, except for the one behind Samson. Ferriday didn't have a prayer of getting out through that one.

"I know you two fellas have a lot to talk over," Fargo said. "I think I'll just go wait outside, if that's all right with you, Samson."

Samson nodded. "It's all right. This won't take me long."

Fargo closed the door as he went outside. He stood on the boardwalk in front of Ferriday's office and leaned back against the wall.

Within seconds it got noisy inside. Fargo heard bumps, smacks, and groans.

The groans didn't sound as if they came from Samson.

A woman passed by, and Fargo politely touched the brim of his hat.

"Is there trouble here?" she said.

"Just somebody doing a little work in the office," Fargo said, as something slammed into the wall behind him. "It'll be done soon."

The woman gave him a skeptical look and hurried on her way.

After another couple of minutes, Samson opened the door and came outside. He pulled the door closed and smoothed down the front of his pants as if to clean his hands. Fargo saw that his knuckles were scraped, but he didn't appear to have sustained any other damage.

"You ready to go?" Samson asked.

Fargo pushed himself off the wall with one foot. "I'm ready. How's Ferriday?"

"I beat the livin' hell out of him."

"He need a doctor?"

"Nah. He'll be all right. Be a sight to see for a while, though. I blacked both his eyes for him."

"Was it better than having your daughters rob stagecoaches?"

Samson grinned. "Damn right it was. You've been right about a lot of things, Fargo."

Fargo didn't see any point in rubbing it

in. He said, "When are you and Kate tying the knot?"

"Won't be long now. You'll have to come to the weddin'."

"I might just do that," Fargo said. "There's one of your daughters says she has a little present for me."

"Which one?"

"Prue."

"What kind of present is it?" Samson said.

It was Fargo's turn to grin. "I guess I'll just have to wait and find out."

"That means you'll be comin' to the weddin', then."

"Yeah," Fargo said. "It does."

"I knew it all along," Samson said.

"How'd you know?"

"Prue told me," Samson said. He clapped Fargo on the back with one big hand. "She said she just had a feelin'."